The characters and events portrayed in this book are fictitious. Any similarity to real persons, living or dead, is coincidental and not intended by the author. Any reference to real locations is only for atmospheric effect, and in no way truly represents those locations.

Copyright © 2022 by Ryan Casey

Cover design by Miblart

All rights reserved.

No part of this book may be reproduced in any form or by any electronic or mechanical means, including information storage and retrieval systems, without written permission from the author, except for the use of brief quotations in a book review.

Published by Higher Bank Books

DAWN OF CHAOS

A Post Apocalyptic EMP Thriller

WORLD WITHOUT POWER
BOOK 1

RYAN CASEY

GET A POST APOCALYPTIC NOVEL FOR FREE

To instantly receive an exclusive post apocalyptic novel totally free, sign up for Ryan Casey's author newsletter at: ryancaseybooks.com/fanclub

CHAPTER ONE

When Bruce Kayleigh woke up on the morning of August 1st, 2022, he had no idea that today was the day he was going to die.

He clutched onto the cyclic of the helicopter and tried to stop this flying chunk of metal from falling to pieces in mid-air. The wind outside was strong as hell and kept on bashing against the sides of the helicopter, making it rock like a boat on choppy waters. Fear gripped Bruce. He'd heard the news doing the rounds that bad storms were on the way. Freak flooding expected across Britain, apparently, and winds unlike any the country had ever seen. There were talks of stocking up on supplies and panic buying. Climate change is a bitch, and all that—especially since it was supposed to be summer.

But stupidly, he'd dismissed it. He didn't think it'd affect him all that much. He'd done so many flights over the years that he felt kind of invincible to shit like that. Stronger and wiser than the elements.

How wrong he'd been.

He gripped the cyclic tight and tried to steady his course.

All around, warning lights flashed.

Beeping filled the cockpit, echoed around his head.

He just wanted the noise to go away.

He just wanted all this shit to go away...

He glanced over his shoulder at the package lying on the helicopter's floor, and his stomach sank.

Drugs. Piles and piles of drugs. Cocaine, to be specific. Smuggled in from the Netherlands, where it'd made its way up from Nigeria, Peru, Colombia, and Bolivia.

Fuck. He always knew this gig would catch up with him one day. He didn't do it because he *enjoyed* doing it. He knew the risks. But what choice did he have, really? He'd been in prison for domestic assault and armed robbery. Nobody would take him on, and the jobs that *would* take him on were nowhere near worth considering.

And when he was inside, a cellmate called Ronald offered him a job. Flying drugs across the globe. Safe, he told him. Well, as safe as any smuggling operation could be. And good pay, too. Real good pay.

Initially, Bruce refused. He wanted to try to carve a better life for himself when he got out of prison.

He tried to stay clean. Tried to live on the straight and narrow. But it was difficult. And when times got *really* difficult, he kept on going back to that offer and how he wished he'd taken it.

But of course, Ronald was gone. And the offer was gone. So he had to just move on. Get on with his life. With the path he'd chosen.

And then, the strangest thing happened.

Sitting in a café in Manchester Airport.

Who walks out?

Ronald.

They get talking. Reminisce about their time inside like they're chatting about some holiday or something.

And then they get onto the topic of flying.

Of Ronald needing a new pilot.

Sometimes in life, things just fall into place in ways you could never predict.

Besides, he had a talent.

A talent for flying planes. For flying helicopters. For traversing some of the most dangerous routes in the world in the worst conditions. He'd flown everywhere. And while these journeys were always nerve-wracking, he always made it. Always.

A bit of rain and wind on the run from the Netherlands back into Manchester?

Not gonna be a problem.

He was beginning to regret that arrogance.

He turned the cyclic ever so slightly. Took a few breaths as he did. "Come on, Bruce. You've dealt with worse shit than this before. Way, way worse shit."

Another large gust of wind battered the helicopter.

The cyclic slipped from Bruce's grip.

He tumbled to his left, banging his head on the glass.

Hard.

Pain split through his head. And fear crept up through his body, too. He was a calm guy. He'd been through some shit in his life. He was regularly beaten as a kid. And he was bullied at school too. But he never fought back. He never stood up for himself. 'Cause Mum always told him there'd be trouble if he fought back. That he had to stay calm, or bad things would happen to him.

But then, he wondered how sound that advice from Mum was, seeing as she'd been killed by Dad in the end. Punched her a little too hard. Gave her a bleed on the brain. Went to prison. And sparked a need for revenge in Bruce that would define his life.

He remembered the first petty crimes he committed. Stealing sweets from the newsagents and hoping it would be bad enough to get him arrested so he could get to Dad.

Swearing at old people and hoping they'd report him to the police.

But nothing seemed to work.

Nothing got him locked up.

Even stabbing Peter Hayley in the eye with a pencil in maths class only got him suspended from school for two weeks.

It was only when he reached his late teens and started dealing drugs and robbing houses that he finally found a purpose in life—and a backup plan, too.

He was caught on a job on his eightieth burglary. Old guy in his eighties. Had a load of expensive jewellery, presumably his dead wife's. Bruce would never forget sneaking into that bedroom and finding the jackpot—gold, platinum, diamonds—only to turn around and see the old bloke standing there, right in front of him. Tears rolling down his cheeks. Shaking like a leaf.

"Please," the old dude begged. "My Cindy's stuff. Please. It's—it's all I have left of her."

And at that moment, standing there, something shifted inside Bruce. Call it a moral epiphany or whatever the hell you want, but something happened.

And he found he couldn't carry out that burglary.

He just couldn't do it.

So he did the weirdest fucking thing.

He turned himself in.

And then he'd stayed right there in the old geezer's house and waited for the police to arrive.

The old man even made him a brew. Sat with him. Showed him old photos of his wife while his emaciated old cat nudged its head at Bruce's feet. Even shook hands when the blue lights arrived and took him away.

Yeah. The weirdest damned night of his life.

Made even weirder when Bruce found out the old guy was fucking him around all along. His wife, Cindy, was still alive. She was just on holiday in Tenerife for two weeks.

Wankers, the pair of them.

The courts found him guilty of a whole string of offences. And in the end, Bruce didn't mind. He really didn't give a shit. Because at least going to prison meant he could reconnect with his life's goal. His life's dream.

Getting the revenge on his father he'd craved for so many years.

Only... perhaps Bruce was naive. But of course, they didn't throw him in the same prison as his dad. Which made his time inside a kind of hell. Waiting to get out. Trying to figure out how on earth he would get to his dad if he never got a chance to see him again.

And then it all happened one day. A fight. Someone swiped his face with a razor over cigarettes or some shit. He ended up in the infirmary, then had to go to hospital because they were worried about infection.

He remembered lying there in that hospital bed and then seeing him in the corner of his eye.

Dad.

Working at the hospital.

Working as a cleaner.

They'd looked at one another. Dad was older than he remembered. And he didn't look anywhere near as menacing as he did in his childhood memories, either.

But there he was.

The man who'd made his childhood a nightmare.

The man who'd murdered Mum.

Standing there in the same room as him.

Breathing the same air as him.

And what'd Bruce done?

How did he react?

He didn't.

He just lay there.

Frozen to the spot.

Unable to make a goddamned move.

Dad walked away.

He never saw him again.

Never heard a thing about him again.

To this day, he was still searching for him.

He dragged himself back into his chair. Tightened his grip around the cyclic. The wind howled against the helicopter, making it wobble from side to side. The warning lights flashed. Alarm noises cried out.

And as Bruce sat there, he felt as weak and defenceless and at the mercy of life itself as he had at that moment in that hospital bed.

Frozen.

Unmoving.

Dead.

He squinted out into the darkness at the rain lashing against the glass. He swore he could hear a breeze inside, which was not good news.

And as he hurtled towards the earth, trying to get this helicopter under control, his greatest regret was that he hadn't got up from that hospital bed that day.

That he hadn't walked over to Dad.

Grabbed him.

Looked him right in the eye and seen the fear on his face.

Because that would've been enough for him.

Dad's fear of him would've been more than enough.

He closed his eyes as tears rolled down his face.

"I'm sorry, Mum," he muttered. "I'm sorry I couldn't make it right. I'm sorry I couldn't make him pay. I'm..."

And then, something weird happened.

A bright light.

A flash, so bright it seared through Bruce's closed eyes, forcing him to open them and then shut them again right away just to hide from the glow.

He heard a loud ringing sound.

Piercing, right in his ears.

What the hell was that?

Had he crashed?

He opened his eyes, just a little, to try and see what the fuck was going on.

And that's when, in all the chaos, time stood still.

A green light.

A beautiful green light.

Dancing across the pitch-black darkness outside.

He looked at that bright green glow, and he smiled. He couldn't help it. Because maybe it was the rapid descent, and maybe it was the shock and the emotion of everything that was happening, but it looked beautiful. It looked so damned beautiful.

And then something else struck him.

The warning lights of the helicopter had died.

The alarm sounds had stopped ringing.

In fact... there were no sounds at all.

No sounds of the rotors.

No sound of anything.

Just... falling.

Silent falling.

Gliding through the sky.

Bruce's stomach jolted like he was going down a big drop on a rollercoaster. And at that moment, a wave of gratitude slammed against him. Gratitude for life itself. He hadn't had the best life. He wished he'd had it better.

But being able to live at all?

That was something to be so grateful for.

He was just now realising it, right in his final moments.

He stared up at that beautiful green glow in the sky above him.

Gripped on to the cyclic for dear life, as he tumbled towards the earth.

Smiled.

"I forgive you, Dad," he said as tears streamed down his face. "I—I forgive—"

An explosion ripped through the helicopter.

Intense heat engulfed Bruce.

Agony ripped from head to toe.

He let out a spontaneous, agonised cry.

And then there was nothing.

When Bruce Kayleigh woke up on the morning of August 1st, 2022, he had no idea that today was the day he was going to die.

Nobody did.

But as darkness descended on the globe, he wouldn't be the first.

And he certainly wouldn't be the last.

CHAPTER TWO

Earlier that day...

If Sam knew how the rest of the day was going to unfold, he would most definitely have stayed at home.

He sat in the middle of the traffic jam and honked his horn. The cars ahead of him stood at a complete standstill. Why? It was raining a bit. Yes, the floods were meant to be bad, according to the news. And it was a little bit windy, sure.

But the real problem here?

Hysteria.

The news was stirring up some kind of bullshit about the "worst storms ever seen." They always did that, right? Every frigging storm was the worst storm the media had seen, because that's what sold stories and got clicks online. And besides, the fact that these storms were hitting in the middle of August just made even more headlines—just added to the drama.

There was no reason for this hysteria. The same as that hysteria over bloody toilet rolls at the start of the coronavirus pandemic. Toilet rolls? Seriously? Like, what's the worst that can happen if you run out of toilet roll? You have to, God forbid, use kitchen roll for a while? Or take a shower? God help us.

No, all this was nonsense. Panic buying. Mass hysteria stirred up by the media, as per usual.

And it pissed Sam right the hell off.

Especially because he had somewhere to be.

Somewhere very urgent.

He looked out the window at the apocalyptic grey skies. They were *very* grey, to be fair. It was early afternoon, but it kind of felt like night already. Rain lashed down from above, banging against the roof of his Land Rover. Up ahead, a long line of cars, completely at a standstill. Everyone heading into town. Well, *city* technically. But Prestonians were very set in their ways about calling it "town". Old habits died pretty hard, it turned out.

Sam looked at the crowds trying to beat this storm, and he shook his head. What the hell were they going to do when they got to town anyway? What the hell did they know about the sort of supplies to gather in case of emergency? The vast majority of people didn't have a clue how to react in a time of real crisis. They'd have no chance whatsoever. They didn't know about the sorts of foods to stock up on to last them. Most of them didn't even know what to do with food if it didn't come in a microwavable pack or with a Uber Eats label slapped on top of it. They wouldn't have a goddamned Scooby which foods they should really stock up on—the holy grail of peanut butter and wholewheat crackers, or to go for smaller multipacks of cereal rather than big boxes to stop them going staler after opening. Just little tricks like that, which the vast majority of folk didn't have a clue about.

And could he blame them?

The media didn't teach them shit like that.

It taught them about scrolling social media feeds, about Love Island, and feeling depressed because you don't look quite as good as the next person in your filtered selfie.

The media trained depression.

Not resourcefulness.

Not survival.

That shit was unfashionable.

Depression was fashionable as fuck.

Sam looked at his watch. Three o'clock. Shit. He said he'd be there to pick him up at two. He knew they'd probably be ringing him, but they could ring the hell away because he didn't carry his phone around everywhere with him. It pissed him off. Seeing people glued to their screens—even crossing the road while staring into that endless stream of information. He saw something once. Some art exhibit that displayed a bunch of people looking down at their phones. Only the artist had removed the phones, so they were staring at their empty palms instead.

And where did he see this exhibit?

The internet.

Staring at his own bloody phone.

The irony wasn't lost on him.

He glanced at his watch again. One minute past three. Practically the same as it was when he'd last looked a literal frigging minute ago. His stomach sank. He couldn't keep waiting around like this. What was the hold up?

He slammed his fist into the horn again and held it there.

The horn blared.

So loud it started setting other cars off.

Making more of that queue slam on the horns, too.

And he knew it was pointless. He knew it was absolutely frigging futile.

But he had somewhere he needed to be.

And these bastards were holding him up.

These bastards were—

A bang.

Against his right window.

Sam jumped. Let go of the horn. Whoever it was at his window, they'd really made him bloody jump.

He looked around.

A man stood at the window. Tall, muscular type. The kind that spends half their life in the gym and the other half on meal prep, ensuring they got their "macros" and all that bullshit. The kind of bloke Sam really wasn't keen on.

He looked soaking wet. Absolutely drenched in rain.

And he looked angry.

Really angry.

"The hell's your problem?" he shouted.

Sam felt a sense of irritation creeping up inside. He didn't want some jumped-up gym boy coming up to *his* car and banging on *his* window and then having the audacity to ask what *his* problem was. He was thirty-six years old. Way too old for this shit.

So he rolled the window down.

"Do you mind not banging on my window?" Sam said. "You're getting protein powder all over it."

The gym boy frowned. "What the hell?"

Sam shook his head. "Nothing."

He kind of hoped the gym boy might give up. Might walk away. 'Cause Sam wasn't exactly a scrawny git himself. He'd got ripped through other means than the gym. The army required it of him.

"We're all here in this shit together," Gym Boy said. Still here, remarkably. "What the hell do you think you're trying to achieve by slamming on your horn and pissing everyone else off?"

A knot grew in Sam's chest. He closed his eyes, took a deep breath. Tried to keep himself calm. Keep himself cool. He knew he shouldn't have engaged this prick. "Can you just get back to your car? If that traffic starts moving now, then I don't want to be stuck here for another second—"

"Absolute dickhead," Gym Boy said. "It's people like you who give our country a bad name. Fucking prick."

Gym Boy started walking away.

Back across the flooded streets towards his car in front.

And Sam knew he should hold off.

He knew he shouldn't antagonise this prick any more than he already had.

But he wasn't being upstaged by a steroid-head in a shirt that looked like it'd shrunk in the wash.

Especially not after what he'd just said to him.

You give our country a bad name...

He gritted his teeth.

"Screw it," he said.

And then he slammed on the horn again.

Gym Boy stopped.

He turned around.

Looked at Sam through narrowed eyes.

The vein on his right temple bulged and throbbed like an alien trapped inside him, desperate to burst out.

"Bad idea," Gym Boy said, cracking his knuckles. "Very bad idea."

He walked over towards Sam's car, and he looked ready for a fight.

And there was something inside Sam that *wanted* a fight.

Some part, deep inside him, that *wanted* a confrontation.

That wanted...

The gunshots.

The cries.

The screams.

The intense heat and the taste of blood.

Please help us! Please!

Sam's body filled with dread.

He felt frozen.

Frozen to his seat.

He was there again.

In the memory again.

Don't leave me! Don't leave me! Don't...

A gunshot.

Blood.

Dead eyes—

And then the next thing he knew, he felt someone wrapping their hands around his throat.

Dragging him out of his car.

Throwing him onto the flooded street.

He opened his eyes, and he saw Gym Boy above him. Holding on to his neck. Squeezing, tight. Staring down at him, rain falling from his dark hair.

"You piss me off one more time," Gym Boy said. "I dare you to piss me off one more damned time."

And Sam knew he shouldn't antagonise this prick.

He could see from the look in his eyes that he was unhinged.

But as he stared up at him, he could still hear something.

The voices.

The voices in his head.

The screaming.

The crying.

The gunshot and that haunting stare.

"You understand?" Gym Boy shouted. "Tell me. Tell me you understand and that you're gonna get back in your car and be a good, well-behaved boy."

He looked up at Gym Boy as a few people wandered over, covering their mouths with their hands, shocked at what they were witnessing. But most people just ignored the scene. Looked away, pretended they hadn't noticed. The classic British response, right?

Sam spat out some rainwater and blood onto the road beside him.

"Go to hell, roid head," he said. "The size of your muscles won't make up for the size of your minuscule dick."

And then he spat in his face.

Gym Boy's eyes widened.

He wiped the blob of spit from his face.

Looked down at Sam with bloodshot, angry eyes.

"You'll regret that," he said.

And then he pulled back his fist.

Cracked Sam across the face.

Hard.

Pain split through Sam's skull.

His ears started ringing.

But as he lay there in the pouring rain, absolutely soaked to the bone, Sam felt relief.

The pain brought relief.

Because the pain chased the voices away.

The memories away.

The pain chased it all away.

Gym Boy punched him one more time.

And then he stood up and walked away without saying another word.

Left Sam lying there on the side of the road.

Rain hammering down.

People rushing over to see if he was okay.

And the traffic, moving now.

Slowly but surely moving, circumnavigating their way around his car, which was now the one causing the obstruction.

Honking at it to move.

He lay there, shook his head, and he smiled.

Because at least the memories were gone.

At least they'd all gone away again.

For now.

CHAPTER THREE

Tara knew she was in trouble when she heard the front door click open.

Shit. Shit, shit, shit. He wasn't supposed to be home yet. He was supposed to be going out for beers with the boys tonight, even if it was stormy as hell out there, and going out was a terrible idea. The news reports had been warning of severe storms on the horizon, the likes of which the country had never seen. There were whispers of mass food shortages and the army being drafted in to help with the inevitable disarray.

But typically, Tara hadn't really thought much of it. Had anyone? It was exactly the same as when the first murmurings of Covid-19 emerged. Nobody knew it would take off in the way it did. People didn't think it would affect them until they were literally being thrown into lockdown—and then they pretended to be shocked like they never saw it coming.

You'd think humanity would learn its lesson, wouldn't you?

And looking outside the window right now, Tara had to admit she'd never quite seen anything like it here in the UK.

The rain was lashing down heavily from those charcoal grey skies. Water splashed up from the waterlogged streets. A fast-flowing stream ran down the road, and that stream was threatening to turn into a river any time soon. A couple wandered down the street, hand in hand, trying to push a pram along and having a hard time of it. But even they didn't look too alarmed, even though the wind and the rain were battering them. They were smiling. Laughing.

It made Tara think of the life she could have had.

The life she always wanted.

Tara heard the door click shut, and she knew she wasn't imagining things.

He was here.

He was really home.

And that thought filled her with dread.

She looked down at the letter in front of her. The letter she'd just finished writing. The plan was to get that letter written, and then… well, what was the plan once the letter was written? She had a vague idea of what she was going to do next. She'd been planning towards this weekend for weeks now—and a storm wasn't going to stop her. She was going to leave the letter on the table in the middle of their two-bedroom flat—well, Jonno's two-bedroom flat. And then she was going to get a bus into town, then a train to Lancaster, and then a train from there over to Arnside, where she could find her parents and stay with them for a while.

The thought made her feel a little sick. The thought of seeing her parents after all these years. The thought of what they'd say. Of how they'd judge her. Just like they'd judged her for her entire life…

Of how differently they looked at her since…

She took a deep breath.

What other choice did she have?

Where else could she go?

She didn't have any friends left. Jonno had seen to that.

She didn't have anyone else she could go to.

She didn't have a job. Her nursing training was proving "too stressful," according to Jonno, so he'd encouraged her to give that dream up. He had a flat, after all, and he could foot the bill.

Hell, she didn't even have a car anymore.

Thirty years old, and she'd lost everything.

And she hadn't even realised she'd sleepwalked right into this misery.

She sat there and listened to the footsteps start creaking upstairs towards the living room she was sitting in like she was watching it all unfold in a movie, not in reality.

And she knew she needed to do something.

She couldn't just sit here and wait.

She had to act.

She snatched the letter she'd just spent the last four hours poring over. Crumpled it up in her hand and looked around the room. Looked for somewhere she could hide it. First instinct was to bin it. But she knew Jonno always checked the bins. He didn't trust her because of the time he'd found a number a guy had given to her on a night out in the rubbish. Told her she was careless for accepting it and that she should've told him where to shove it—or to ring him and he'd come and sort the bloke out.

That was the beginning of the end of Tara's friendships. In the end, it just wasn't worth Jonno's insecurity, his sulking, anymore.

She always prided herself on being strong. On being tough. Her whole life, she'd been a fighter.

But she had no idea how she'd wandered into her world being so damned small.

But one thing was for sure.

She needed to do something right now.

Because Jonno was home.

Footsteps creaked further and further up the stairs, closer towards her.

She felt sick. Shaky. He wasn't supposed to be home yet. This wasn't how things were supposed to go.

She took a deep breath.

Keep your shit together, Tara. Keep it all together.
You're strong. And you aren't gonna get anywhere by moping.
You've never got anywhere by moping.
Think.
Just think.

She looked around as those footsteps edged closer and saw the CD rack in the corner of the lounge.

Jonno liked buying CDs. He was a bit of a weirdo like that. One of the quirks that attracted her to him in the first place. Because CDs were such a weird one to still collect, right? Vinyl, sure. They had an ancient quality to them that made them stand out.

But CDs...

Hell, the more Tara thought about it, the more she should've seen it as a red flag from the off.

But right now, these CDs stood out to her.

Right now, she was grateful for Jonno's weird CD habit.

Because she saw one of her CDs on top from back in her uni days. A Frank Ocean album. She'd showed it to Jonno once, but he just wasn't having any of it, and claimed it was trash—even if critics generally regarded it as one of the decade's best albums. It was like that with anything Tara had a strong opinion on. He seemed to revel in belittling her, usually subtly, but progressively more assertively these days. He got power from undermining her opinions.

But if there was one place Jonno wasn't going to look, it was in that Frank Ocean CD case.

Footsteps creaked further up the staircase.

He was so close now.

Tara ran across the lounge.

Tumbled over, almost losing her footing.

She staggered back to her feet, then over towards that CD rack.

Grabbed the Frank Ocean CD.

Footsteps right outside the door now.

She opened the CD case with shaky hands.

Stuffed the scrunched-up note in there.

And then she closed the CD.

Threw it back on top of the rack.

The door opened.

Tara turned around.

Jonno walked into the room.

He smiled at her. He was drenched. The vein on his temple popped out like it always seemed to when he'd been going hard at the gym.

Or when he was angry.

And right now, his black muscle-fit clothes were sodden, and he was dripping all over the new carpet they'd had put in just a couple of months ago—the carpet Tara paid for. "*It's about time you contributed something to this place,*" he'd said. "*Seeing as I've been letting you live here rent-free.*"

"Hello, love," he said. "It's a nightmare out there. How's your day been?"

He walked over towards her, his rain-sodden boots squelching with every step.

And Tara felt totally frozen.

Which made her feel totally pathetic.

Because she was a woman.

A strong adult woman who prided herself on her independence.

Who'd had to fight—who'd had to show strength and courage —all her life.

And yet here she was.

Fearing someone.

Fearing a *man*.

"The rain's worse than they said it was gonna be. And you know how much they've been whinging about it, so that's saying something. You okay?"

He stopped right in front of her.

Stared into her eyes with those big blue eyes of his.

She wanted to tell him it was over.

She wanted to find the strength she knew she had inside her and tell him she was going.

That it was done.

That she was finished with his put-downs.

That she was done with how belittling he could be.

That she wanted her friends back.

Her life back.

"Tara?" Jonno said. "What's wrong?"

But in the end, all she could do was lower her head and smile.

"Nothing," she said. "I just... I just feel a bit shitty, that's all. Coming down with something, I think."

Jonno narrowed his eyes and shook his head. And then he walked towards her, wrapped his arms around her, a little too tight for comfort—just tight enough that it squeezed the air from her lungs.

"Bless you," he said. "I told you; you need to start eating healthier. I'm not saying you're unhealthy. I mean, we all put on a bit of weight at some point, right? But the sooner you can shake it off, the better you'll feel. Hmm?"

She felt ashamed hearing those words.

How dare he.

How dare he belittle her like that.

She knew she wasn't fat. Nowhere near.

And even if she was, she was still an attractive woman.

Right?

"Don't you worry," he said, squeezing tighter. "I'm here now. We're going to be okay. Everything's going to be okay."

Behind them, neither of them heard the Frank Ocean CD case pop open as the scrunched-up breakup letter unfurled itself, slowly, quietly...

CHAPTER FOUR

Sam dragged himself to his feet and hurled himself through the pools of water towards his car.

He felt like shit. Which went without saying really, considering he'd just been dragged out of his car and punched in the face. A bunch of people gathered around him, asking if he was okay. But he waved them off 'cause he couldn't really be doing with them right now. All things considered, he'd antagonised the prick. In a way, he'd asked for it.

Weirdly, he'd *wanted* it.

He'd *deserved* it.

The sound of screaming.

The crack of gunfire.

The taste of blood...

No.

Don't think about that.

Not right now.

He walked over to his old Land Rover. An old mechanical diesel model with none of that computerised nonsense. He saw the way the world was going when it came to integrating electronics and computers into cars. Recently, he'd read one company was going to start *charging* a subscription fee for the use of air conditioning. Anything that could be integrated into a car could therefore be switched on and off remotely, and he was absolutely *not* down for any of that shit.

He'd much rather be stuck in a sweltering car without air con than being forced by some corporation to pay a monthly fee for the privilege of slightly cooler air.

The rain really was pretty damned bad, to be honest. Running down the road pretty heavily now. Up ahead, a fountain of dirty brown water was shooting out of a blocked drain. The traffic was moving again, but slowly now. A few people who didn't realise what was going on were pipping their horns at him. Which, in a way, kind of made him want to drag his feet even more.

But hey. Enough antagonising people for one day.

And besides. There was somewhere he needed to be.

Somewhere he *really* needed to be.

Someone he was very late for.

He opened his car door. Sat back inside. He was drenched. Completely soaked to the bone. Rain pounded down even heavier than before on his car roof. His windscreen was a waterfall that he could barely see through.

He shook his head and went to start up the car.

The engine coughed, and nothing happened.

Sam's stomach sank. Not now. Not fucking now…

He turned his key.

Got into gear.

Went to accelerate.

And again, the engine just coughed and died.

Sam's stomach sank even frigging more.

He knew he needed to do some work on his Land Rover. It'd been on its last legs for a ridiculous amount of time now. The battery was definitely bust. He'd known about it for weeks now. And yet he'd still been stupid enough to come out here in the middle of a storm only for *this* to happen.

He shook his head. "You're an idiot. An absolute frigging idiot."

He sat there as rain pounded down from above. Cars were driving around him now, the water a quarter of the way up their tyres. Somewhere in the distance, lightning flashed. Shit. This wasn't like Britain. This was like some kind of storm from overseas. Something tropical like a typhoon or a hurricane. Maybe he was wrong to dismiss it as media scaremongering.

He was an idiot for coming out here.

But he'd been an idiot for a reason.

And that reason was sitting waiting for him in the city centre right now.

A mile's walk away.

He tried the car again. Tried to get it going.

But again, the engine just laughed at him.

Again, it coughed, spluttered, and died on him, joining every-damned-thing else in making a mockery of him today.

He knew he was going to have to get the AA out and get it towed. But he figured that might take a hell of a long time in this weather—weather that would only get worse.

He glanced at his watch. Quarter past three now. Which meant he...

And then he noticed something.

A crack. Right across his watch.

His stomach sank. That bastard. That bastard Gym Boy must've cracked it.

He thought about Rebecca.

Thought about the day she'd bought this watch for him as a birthday present.

How happy he felt.

How happy *she* was with that big, beautiful, beaming smile of hers, so happy to see him happy.

He smiled at the memory.

Smiled as he sat there in the pouring rain in his broken-down car, completely alone.

And then that solitude hit him.

Like an emptiness, right in the middle of his chest.

The memory.

The memory that destroyed everything.

"No," he muttered.

He saw the road ahead. A few people running down the pavement, completely drenched in rain. The tall city centre buildings up ahead, about a mile away.

A knot grew in his chest.

His heart started racing.

He wasn't going to sit here and wait to be towed away.

He wasn't going to twiddle his thumbs and wait here, relying on someone else. That'd never been his way. Ever.

He was going to get to the city centre.

And then he was going to go to Jeff's hardware store, find a damned battery, drag it the hell back here, and sort this car out himself.

He took a deep breath, and he shook his head.

The whole reason he had a car that some would call an "old banger" was so he was safe if ever there was some sort of mass power outage. Cars nowadays were so stuffed with computers and machinery and artificial intelligence that if ever a solar flare or an EMP attack occurred, they'd be completely fried.

Nah, give Sam something good, solid, and old-fashioned any day if it meant getting from A to B without the risk of being charged for fucking airbag deployment.

But it's not done a great job of getting you from A to B today, has it?

He shook his head again. Sighed.

"The things we do for love."

On the car dashboard, he saw a little photo staring back at him. A photo of an Alsatian.

A photo of Harvey.

Sam smiled. "I hope you have an idea how much trouble I'm going through to come get you, lad."

And then he opened his car door and stepped out into the torrential rain.

As it turned out, Harvey had absolutely no idea how much trouble Sam was getting into to get him.

Nobody knew how much trouble they were about to be plunged into.

CHAPTER FIVE

Tara stared out at the pouring rain and wondered when Jonno's mood would take a turn for the worse.

Because it always did.

Eventually, it always did.

That was one thing in her life that was depressingly predictable at this stage.

She sat on the sofa with Jonno beside her and watched the rain hammer down outside. The sky was getting greyer and greyer. She thought the news channels might be exaggerating when they'd talked about the worst storms in Britain for decades. But sitting here now, she could see they'd probably had a point all along.

And it made her feel anxious. It made her feel incredibly tense.

Because it meant her opportunity to get away from this place —to leave Jonno, once and for all—was going to be pretty damned difficult.

She wanted to get away. She wanted to escape. As melodramatic as the word "escape" felt, that's really what it felt like now. That's really what she'd been pushed to.

She felt trapped.

She felt suffocated.

She needed to get out of here.

But at the same time... the weather wasn't going to get any better.

And Jonno wasn't leaving her side.

"You haven't touched your prawn toast."

Tara snapped back into the room with a jolt. She looked at Jonno, then down at the prawn toast in front of her. It was dry. Cold. Stale. Jonno loved the Chinese he'd got it from, but Tara had never particularly rated it. He told her it was a matter of taste. That she preferred the "greasy stuff." And that in the long run, this would be better for her.

She wanted to claw his eyes out. And the depressing thing was... once upon a time, she would've done. She wouldn't have taken any shit from anyone a few years ago. Particularly a *man*.

But Jonno had been crafty. So crafty that she'd only really seen what she'd walked right into when it was already too late.

She was besotted with him in the early days. They met in the park. She was waiting for a dental appointment with an abscess the size of a tennis ball and decided to read a book in the park to try and distract her attention from the agony. And out of her periphery wandered this gorgeous, tall, muscular man with a smile to die for.

She remembered her first reaction. Embarrassment. Embarrassment that a man so hot was seeing her in her abscess-riddled state.

But he hadn't even mentioned it. Hadn't even noticed it as far as she could tell. He'd just told her he was walking back from a business meeting about setting up a new gym and told her he really wanted to grab a drink, and before she knew it, she was in bed with him, then moving in with him and... bam. It all happened fast. Really damned fast.

Like a fairytale.

She couldn't pinpoint the first time she'd started getting bad feelings about Jonno. Maybe it was her defensiveness when a few of her friends told her he'd flirted with them, said inappropriate things to them. Jonno was mortified when he found out. Absolutely devastated. Tara had looked into his eyes, and he'd promised her nothing had happened.

And she'd told him it was okay. Because Suzy was a fantasist anyway, and the rest of the girls were in their late twenties and single and probably just jealous that she'd met such a catch.

So naturally, she distanced herself from Suzy. Distanced herself from the rest of her friends.

Slowly but surely.

One by one.

Until there was nothing left.

The distancing from her parents started much earlier before she even met Jonno. They were always pretty suffocating as far as parents went. They always saw her as their little girl, even when she was a teenager, and didn't let her live as free a life as she wanted to live. They encouraged her to study at a university close to home so they could "help her out" rather than spreading her wings and trying her luck living elsewhere. They didn't mean bad. Tara was sure of that. Their intentions were good. And they had their reasons for being rather frosty with her.

But they made her crave freedom. They'd made her want to live a life of her own.

And where had that led her?

Right into the arms of a controlling man-child.

Tara looked down at the pile of prawn toast before her and took a deep breath. "I... I'm not so hungry. Like I said. I don't feel too good."

Jonno's eyes narrowed. For a second, for just a second, he looked pissed off. Like Tara's refusal to eat the prawn toast bothered him somehow. Offended him. Like it was a personal dig at him rather than a simple refusal of some lukewarm seafood stuffed bread. "Is it because of what I said earlier?"

"What?"

"What I said about you needing to shed a few pounds?"

Tara's stomach turned when she heard those words. *Bastard.* How dare he double down on it. "No. It's nothing to do with that."

Jonno laughed. Reached over and pinched her arm, a little harder than was comfortable. "Someone's stroppy."

Tara's arm stung where he'd pinched her. She genuinely felt sick now. Her head was spinning. She felt on the verge of snapping. She'd always kept so calm around Jonno. She'd always kept shit so under control.

Because she knew what he could be like if she didn't stay calm.

If she didn't stay under control.

She knew what he'd put her through.

His violence was never physical. Not inappropriately so, anyway.

But it was emotionally draining. His sulking. His words. And his shouting. His temper.

She knew she should get away. She knew she should leave.

But he'd made her feel like she had nobody.

Made her feel like there was nowhere to go.

And then there were the times he was sweet.

The times he laid on the charm. Usually, right after he'd been a dick to her. And when he was sweet, he was *really* sweet. Made her remember what he used to be like. What *they* used to be like as a couple.

And besides. Jonno knew her secret.

He knew the truth about her.

He was the only one who did, really.

And that made him... special, in some way.

Because he hadn't judged her for it.

But things had snapped. She'd cracked. Everything had changed.

This weekend was supposed to be the weekend.

Today was supposed to be the day.

But this storm looked like it was going to hold her back.

And if she didn't get out this weekend... when the hell *would* she get out at all?

"I'm only joking, stroppy," Jonno said, wrapping his arm around her neck, pulling her close. "Want some wine?"

Tara saw the bottle over beside the sofa. Barely touched. She shook her head. "I'm okay."

Jonno squeezed tighter. There was no love in his embrace. It felt cold. Like a headlock. A reminder that physically, he was stronger than her. And he was keen to remind her of that, however subtly, as often as he possibly could. "Just think. This storm's in for the weekend at the very least, apparently. You and me, right here with each other. Nobody going anywhere..."

He moved his hand onto her thigh.

She felt sick.

Her face went hot.

She jolted away.

Stood up.

Only when she reacted did she realise what she'd done.

She saw the look in Jonno's eyes.

The redness on his face.

The embarrassment.

The confusion.

The anger.

"Tara?" he said.

Tara's heart raced. She could barely breathe. She couldn't stay here. She had to get out of this room.

But she had to be careful about it, too.

She took as deep a breath as she possibly could. Tightened her fists. "I—I'm sorry. I just... Let me just go to the bathroom, okay?

Splash my face a little? And then... and then I'll be right back with you."

Jonno stared at her.

Started right into her eyes.

His jaw tensed and twitched.

And Tara knew this wasn't going to be good.

The prospect of being stuck in here with a sulking Jonno was more than she could bear.

And then his face turned.

He smiled.

Nodded.

"Sure, love. Sure. You go get yourself freshened up. I'll be right here."

A wave of relief crashed over Tara.

She wasn't expecting that level of mercy. Not one bit.

She nodded back at him.

Turned around.

Walked away, through the spare bedroom of her flat, towards the bathroom, as thunder erupted outside and rain hammered down on the roof.

It might only be a moment.

But it was a moment she needed.

One thing was for sure.

She was not staying in this house for the weekend.

She was not staying here with Jonno much longer.

She was getting out of here.

Today.

BACK IN THE LOUNGE, Jonno saw the little scrunched-up ball of paper tumble to the floor out of that Frank Ocean CD case...

CHAPTER SIX

Prime Minister Pamela Morton stared at the briefing screen before her and tried to wrap her head around everything Defence Secretary Pritchard was telling her.

But how the hell did anyone respond when they were told everything was on the verge of falling apart, all in a heartbeat?

"You need to decide how we're going to act, Prime Minister," Pritchard said. "Whether we warn people. Whether we prepare them for what's about to happen. Or whether we trust our military to deliver. Follow Plan A."

Pamela felt sick. Her head felt completely engulfed in thick fog. She'd spent the week chairing COBRA meetings about the impending storms. Extreme weather events the likes of which the nation hadn't seen for some time—if ever. And they were weather events that were going to batter the entire country far harder than she'd dared admit. From the streets of London to the rural Lake District, these winds and the floods that would follow would cause much damage, both literal and economical, and also cost lives. Many lives.

And yet... that was only the tip of the iceberg.

Compared to what she was discovering right now—what she was being briefed on right now—it was nothing.

She sighed. The taste of cigarettes was strong on her breath. She'd given up smoking eight years ago as a part of a healthy image campaign that came with the territory of running for office. Officially, anyway. Truth was, she smoked more in office than she'd ever done. Stress did that to a person.

And her stress levels had been through the roof the last few weeks.

She took another deep breath. Tried to calm herself. Tried to remain composed. "And you're saying… you're saying there's no way we can keep the power online?"

Pritchard shook her head. Stared at Pamela's feet. And that really caught Pamela's attention. Em Pritchard was one tough cookie. A defence secretary who took her job very, very seriously. She'd run against Pamela for leader eight years ago, and things had been nasty between them. A nastiness that grew into mutual respect over time.

Pamela had never seen Em looking so broken. Looking so… weak.

It must be serious if even she looked distraught.

If she couldn't look Pamela in the eye.

"And—and the chances of this solar flare doing what you've told me?"

Pritchard looked up. Glanced right into Pamela's eyes, just for a second.

"Not 100%," she said. "But not much lower than 90% either."

Pamela felt like she'd been punched.

Everything Pritchard had just told her spun around her head.

Some talk about a solar storm on the sun. The calls from NASA overseas about an imminent solar flare, larger and stronger than any in history. The way she'd rolled her eyes when she'd first got the call because it was late, and she didn't understand how a solar flare could be such an emergency because the sun was millions of miles away, and besides, solar flares that wiped out the power were the work of science fiction, weren't they?

But this solar flare was different.

This solar flare was the kind that would batter the Earth's surface.

That would leave the world in darkness.

And not just the electricity grid either. Not just mains electricity. But battery power.

Phones.

Cars.

Everything.

All gone. All in an instant.

All in a flash.

From light to darkness.

And they barely even had any time to prepare.

Apparently, the global scientific community had been monitoring this impending solar storm for quite some time. Initially, predictions were that the event might take out power in Alaska and eastern Russia, but nothing particularly major. There were a few alarmist reports, as always. But at the end of the day, if you listened to every alarmist report when in government, you'd never find the time to govern.

But it seemed like those noisy alarmists were right.

"And—and what backup plans do we have?" Pamela said. "For —for getting the power back online?"

Pritchard couldn't look her in the eye.

Again, she stared down at the floor.

"Em," Pamela said. Her voice shaking far more than she wanted it to right now. "I'm asking you as a person. Not as a defence secretary, but as someone who's known you for years. Who's sparred with you and then befriended you. What backup plans do we have?"

Pritchard looked up at her now. And Pamela could tell from the look in her eyes that the answer wasn't good.

"We don't... We haven't prepared for something like this, Pamela."

Another punch to the gut. "We... we haven't prepared for something like this?"

"We *can't* prepare for something like this," she said, shaking. "We've... The whole world. It's built itself on power. On electricity. On connectivity. It's taken it for granted. And we... we have to begin realising that we can't take it for granted any longer. Because there's a very strong chance we don't have long left."

Pamela's stomach dropped. Fear started to grow. The questions she was asking were questions she didn't want to ask—but questions she knew she had to. "How—how much longer do we have?"

Pritchard scratched her arms. "About... about an hour."

An hour.

"And then it's over," Pamela said. "Everything... everything's over?"

Pritchard took a shaky breath. Pamela swore she saw a tear rolling down her cheek. "If I were you—and I'm speaking to you as a friend—I would follow the military to safety and shelter immediately. With your family. I would follow their protocols. Because we have accounted for that. The military will take to the streets as soon as the outage occurs. They're already on the streets because of the floods and the storms. They'll do what they can for people. And in time... in time, this nation will stand tall again. But this is going to change everything, Pamela. This is going to change life as we know it. Forever. We might be government now. But we mean nothing without power. We have no power without power."

Pamela stood there in the middle of the cabinet office. Outside, she heard the thunderstorms. She saw the rain hammering down from the dark grey skies.

And a tear rolled down her cheek.

"A ninety-percent chance, you say?" Pamela asked.

Pritchard nodded. "Give or take."

She looked up at those grey skies, and she prayed to God that the odds would fall in their favour and that the 10% would reign supreme, not for the first time in history.

"Let's hope the odds are in our favour today," she said.

She was about to find out very soon.

CHAPTER SEVEN

Sam didn't think today could get any worse than being dragged out of his car in the middle of a fucking enormous storm and being punched in the face by a gym boy meat-head.

But he was wrong about that.

Very wrong.

He sat on the hard plastic chair in the middle of this busy waiting room. He was absolutely drenched, dripping onto the floor. He could taste blood on his lips. Some of the other punters in here kept on looking over at him, muttering to each other disapprovingly. Which didn't totally surprise him. They were all posh old gits in here. He hated this place, but he knew they had a good reputation, and he only wanted the best for Harvey at the end of the day. And besides, the vet he saw—Emma—was really, really good. Only person he'd trust putting his pup under general anaesthetic, that was for sure.

He missed Harvey. He'd only been here a couple of days, and he had to admit life wasn't the same without him. He was only in for a fairly routine tooth extraction, but they wanted to keep him in overnight to make sure he recovered okay, which no doubt added an extra hundred quid to his bill.

But hey. Where Harvey was concerned, his safety was paramount.

The bright artificial lights were giving him a headache. He just wanted to get his dog and get the hell out of the city and back home before this storm got any worse.

He'd left his Land Rover by the side of the road about a mile back, just outside the centre. His plan was to grab a battery for it from Jeff's hardware store when he was done here, then get it started and drive it back home. Sure, that wouldn't be easy, not in this storm. But at the end of the day, he believed the only way he could do a good job was if he did it himself.

And with the amount of time he'd been waiting for the vets to call his name so he could collect Harvey, he was starting to think if he might've been able to do his surgery better himself, too.

Harvey was his Alsatian. Seven years old now. He'd always been a dog person. Had dogs all his life, right from being a kid. His first friend was a Golden Labrador called Chad. And his first heartbreak was Chad's death. He'd never forget the way his mum held him. Told him Chad had gone to heaven to play with the other dogs, and he'd be happier than ever there.

And Sam felt so sad about that. He didn't want Chad to be in heaven with the other dogs because Chad always preferred people to dogs. And knowing he was so, so far away from Chad was the source of much discomfort for a young Sam. A discomfort and a disease about bonding with other people that had festered in much of the rest of his life.

A discomfort that probably led him right into the army.

He twitched on his plastic seat. Outside, the wind howled, and cars honked at each other. The water was right up the tyres now. It was bad, actually. Really bloody bad. Sam didn't think it'd be as bad as they were making out on the news, but it looked like it was actually worse.

Still, he didn't get why so many people weren't just staying at home with whatever supplies they had. Then again, they weren't the type to prepare for disaster, the general public. Summed up the British mentality, really. Head in the sand, hope it all goes away, hope everything just fixes itself and figures itself out.

No knowledge of preparing for the worst.

Of stocking up on supplies.

On preparing for disaster.

He knew a thing or two about survival. It'd always been something that'd interested him, right from when he was a kid. Used to enjoy going out camping with his Uncle Roger, building a tent, finding firewood, keeping warm. Some of his best memories were sitting in a tent in the middle of the woods, lighting a fire using one of the many methods he'd learned, feeling the warmth against his face, and falling asleep in the orange glow.

And that interest in survival probably prompted him to join the army. It certainly didn't dampen his interest, that was for sure. He learned a whole host of things there. Different methods of surviving the worst of situations, the harshest of conditions.

But he was surprised how little his colleagues knew about basic things like water filtration, starting fires, hunting, that sort of thing. For that reason, he was something of a novelty to have around. Never short of friends.

A knot tightened in his stomach.

How much things changed...

He glanced at his watch. Four o clock now. He was supposed to be here to pick Harvey up from his surgery a couple of hours ago. But the weather had seen to that. Traffic was always a nightmare heading into town anyway. Part of the reason he escaped to the outskirts.

Mostly to get to somewhere quieter.

But also to get away.

To get away from the memories.

To get away from the past.

He saw that crack on his watch. The crack Gym Boy had given him in the road. He felt his stomach sink upon seeing it. A wave of sadness. That watch meant something to him. It was precious to him. It reminded him of her. Of Rebecca. It reminded him of...

He closed his eyes.

He didn't have to think about her now.

He didn't have to think about how things went.

How things fell apart.

How things—

"Mr Martins?"

Sam opened his eyes.

A woman stood before him. Receptionist. Tall, with long dark hair. Had strict high-school teacher vibes about her, something Sam found immediately rather off-putting. She was always a bit of a witch, that was for sure.

She scanned him from head to toe. Looked down at the water pooling beneath his seat. Somewhere nearby, Sam heard a dog barking and another howling. Much more annoying when it wasn't your own.

"Hi," he said.

"Yeah," the receptionist said. "Slight problem. Harvey's doing well. He's doing fine, really. But we're going to need to keep him in a little longer."

Sam frowned. "A little longer? But you said—"

"We have some..." she scanned him from head to toe again, then back up to his eyes. "Some welfare concerns."

Sam felt a knot tighten in his chest. A ball of anger grew inside him. Welfare concerns? Fucking welfare concerns? No. No fucking way. Harvey was the best exercised, best-loved dog he knew. He was his goddamned world. He'd do anything for him. He'd goddamned *die* for him.

And this posh cow thought she had the right to stand here and patronise him because... because why?

Because he looked in a shit way?

Because he wasn't dressed in a fucking three-piece suit to the vets?

No. No, he wasn't having that. He wasn't having that at all.

He cleared his throat. "Excuse me?"

The woman smiled that awful smile these cows always smiled. "We're... somewhat concerned. He needs more teeth extracting than we first suspected. And we believe that if the proper measures had been taken in advance, that he wouldn't be in this predicament right now. Besides. We're... You're bleeding, sir. From your nose. And your mouth. Quite badly. You're not in a good way. And that concerns us. That's all."

Sam couldn't believe what he was hearing.

Anger rose inside him.

His heart started racing harder.

He had to stay cool.

Had to keep things under control.

But he could see the eyes of the waiting room staring over at him.

He could see the judgemental expression on this receptionist's face.

He could see how everyone in here was looking at him like he was some kind of bad guy, even though that wasn't true.

It wasn't true at all.

"This is all because I didn't pay for that dental coverage a year ago, isn't it?"

The receptionist frowned. "Don't be absurd, Mr Martins."

"Let me tell you something," Sam said. "Harvey is well-loved. More loved than any dog I've ever known."

The receptionist tilted her head and did these sad, puppy-dog eyes that had absolutely no sincerity in them whatsoever. Like she was trying to pretend she understood when in fact, she'd already made her mind up. "I don't doubt you love him. We all love our dogs... in our own ways."

Sam gritted his teeth.

The anger intensifying.

The sound of those barking and howling dogs growing louder.

The rainfall so hard on this roof.

The artificial lights so bright.

And the eyes.

The eyes of everyone, staring right at him like *he* was the one in the wrong here.

"That dog is my world," Sam said. "My absolute world. Ever since…"

No.

Don't think about that.

Not now.

The receptionist stepped over to Sam. She stood right in front of him. Looked right into his eyes.

And then she reached out and put a hand on his shoulder.

"I am sorry, Mr Martins. But we are going to have to keep Harvey in. Until we've truly established he is fit to leave with you. So for now… either you can wait here and cause a scene. Or you can go home. And wait for our call. It shouldn't be much longer."

Sam felt his anger intensifying.

His heart racing.

His head spinning.

He knew he had to keep shit under control.

He knew he couldn't take any chances.

But…

He tightened his fists.

"You can say whatever you goddamned want to," Sam said. "I'm here for my dog. Right now. And I'm not leaving without him."

The receptionist's eyes widened.

The waiting room went deathly silent.

And for a moment, just a moment, Sam swore he saw the receptionist smile.

"Very well," she said.

She walked back over to reception.

Went behind the desk.

And for a moment, Sam thought she might legitimately be going to have a word with the vet about letting Harvey home with him.

But she did something else.

She picked up the phone.

Dialled.

Waited a few seconds, staring at Sam.

Everyone in here staring at Sam like they had nothing better to do.

She waited in silence, and then she spoke.

"Police? This is Oakward Veterinary Practice in Preston City Centre. Yes, we're having a problem with one of our clients. An animal welfare issue, yes. And causing quite a scene. Being rather threatening. Yes. Thanks."

Sam couldn't actually believe what he was hearing.

He couldn't *actually* believe it.

"Really?" he shouted, unable to keep his frustration under wraps any longer. "Is there really any fucking need for that?"

"Sir," the receptionist shouted. "We have guests in here. Children in here."

"I don't give a fuck if the bloody Pope's in here," Sam said. "Harvey is my dog. And there are no bloody welfare issues. So where is he? Tell me where the bloody hell he…"

He wasn't sure if he said another word.

Because above him, all the lights burst.

Every single one of those bright lights went out.

Darkness descended on the vets.

CHAPTER EIGHT

When Tara stepped back into the lounge, she immediately knew something was wrong.

Jonno was standing at the window, staring out at the lashing rain. He had his hands behind his back, and he was still. Very still. A part of her wanted to dash over to the door, run downstairs, and get out of here, taking the opportunity while it was on a plate. But another part of her thought she owed him some kind of explanation.

Because one thing was for sure.

Tara was leaving this flat today.

Extreme weather warning or not, she was out of here.

One way or another.

"Jonno?"

Jonno turned around. Looked at her. Smiled. But his eyes looked bloodshot. Like he'd been crying.

"Hey, angel," he said. "How're you feeling?"

His voice sounded soft. Softer than Tara had heard it in quite some time. She remembered when he used to speak to her like that all the time. When she used to sit in the drive-thru cinema with him, watching whatever shitty nineties movie was on before the power decided to give up and go out. And they didn't care because they were next to each other, eating shit popcorn together. She remembered the times she used to go on walks up the Lakes with him to the most beautiful, scenic places. The laughter she'd had with him when he'd slipped over and covered himself in mud over at Coniston. The happiness she'd felt with him.

It reminded her of what she'd had, how good things *could* be, and why it was so hard to walk away from something like this.

Because sometimes, when things were good, Tara wondered if she was being oversensitive. Because every relationship had its flaws, right? No relationship was perfect.

And then the realisation that leaving would be harder than staying because she'd lose the flat, and she was jobless and friendless, and she'd be left with nothing, nothing but crawling back to her parents and relying on them once again—a thought she hated.

She didn't want that. Because she was strong. She was tough.

But enough was enough.

Enough really was enough.

She cleared her throat. Smiled. "Better, actually." Fuck. Where the hell was she going with this? Was she going to tell him the truth today? Or was she going to just get through tonight and see what the weather was like tomorrow? Just typically British, wasn't it? Basing the future on the weather. Just typical. Might as well have a cup of frigging tea just to complete the cliché.

Jonno smiled back at her. "Good. That's good."

He walked over to her. Slowly. She could see this redness to his eyes. Something was off. Something was wrong. Something she couldn't put her finger on.

"You know, I was thinking," he said. "We've been together, what, four years now?"

"Four years. Yeah." Shit. It felt like forever. The whole of her late twenties swallowed up by *this*.

"And I... I've wanted to ask you something. For a long time.

But I've just... I've just never found the perfect moment, you know?"

Oh, God. No. This wasn't happening. This couldn't happen right now.

"What?" Tara asked. Smiling. Trying to keep her composure. Trying to keep her control.

Jonno walked right up to her. Grabbed her hands. Lifted them, kissed them. Tara felt her skin crawl. He gave her the ick. And once someone gave you the ick, there was no going back. "I've been thinking about it for a long time. I've wanted to ask you for a long time. And I... I wanted it to be somewhere nicer than this. Somewhere better than this. Somewhere more romantic."

And then he got down on one knee.

He actually fucking did it.

He reached up

Held her hands.

Stroked them softly, making her skin crawl.

He was doing this.

Oh God, he was actually doing this.

"Tara," he said. "My love. Will you marry me?"

Tara felt a knot in her throat tightening like a vice grip.

A life married to this man flashed before her eyes.

A life growing smaller, and smaller, and smaller.

A life completely subservient to him.

A life that wasn't her own.

She looked down into his eyes, and she took a deep breath.

And then she said something that she knew she had to say.

Something she didn't think she had the strength to say.

But something she knew it was finally, finally time to be honest about.

"I can't," she said.

She expected tears. She expected rage. She expected emotional blackmail and pledges to jump out the window. She expected a tantrum, threats, and all kinds of awful shows of manipulation before hoping she'd just fall back into his grasp when she realised she didn't have anything left.

What she didn't expect was his smile.

A smug, bitter smile.

He got back to his feet.

The vein on his right temple throbbing, pulsating.

"At least you're being honest," he said. "And not a cowardly little snake, like usual."

Fear filled Tara's body.

He'd said awful things to her in the past.

But there was something different about the way he was speaking to her right now.

Something different about the snarl on his face.

There was something seriously *off* about him.

Something she didn't recognise about him.

"Jonno, I'm sorry. But I just don't..."

And then she saw it.

The letter.

In his shaking hands.

He looked down at it, and he shook his head and puffed out his lips. "'Dear Jonno,'" he said.

Tara wanted the world to open beneath her feet. "Jonno. Don't do this—"

"'I didn't want things to end this way. And I don't even know what I'm going to write. There are so many things I could write about. The good times. Because there were good times. The holidays we had in France and the walks we went on. That weekend in Edinburgh where we didn't stop laughing for a solid three days...'"

"Jonno," Tara said. Just wanting this to end. "You've read the letter. You don't have to keep going."

"But I do," Jonno said, snapping the letter away. "You wrote it, right? You wrote the words you wanted to say. So... Actually, why don't you read it?"

Tara's stomach sank. "Don't make me do this."

But then Jonno pushed the letter into her face. "Read it. Read every word."

Tara tried to drag the letter from her face. "Jonno—"

"Read it!"

She jolted back when he shouted like that, and she hated him for it.

She felt tears rolling down her face like the torrential rain outside. She held on to the letter, looked down at it, all crinkled and blotchy with tears.

And then she looked back up at Jonno.

He was crying now. He looked broken. Distraught. But not crying in that emotional blackmail way she'd grown so attuned to. Genuine tears. Like when his grandma died, and she comforted him. She saw a weakness in him. A genuine weakness, like a lost puppy.

"Letter?" he said. "You—you're leaving me by letter? Really?"

And then Tara felt the guilt. She felt like the worst fucking person in the world. That was always the way, wasn't it? One of Jonno's finest abilities. Make her feel like she was awful. Like she was absolutely terrible.

But as guilty as she felt... she was done.

She wasn't getting caught in by his ways anymore.

She tightened her grip around that letter. "I'm not the one who's been abusive."

"Abusive? Get a grip you sensitive bitch. I've given you everything. My home. I've worked for you, to support you. I've given you everything."

"You've taken away my life."

Jonno narrowed his eyes. He shook his head. That vein on his temple was bigger than he'd ever seen it now. "Bitch," he said, a fleck of spit falling onto his chin. "You ungrateful, selfish, narcissistic, jumped up, ugly bitch."

And Tara felt numb. The words should hurt her; she knew

that. But she felt numb. She'd heard it all before. Nothing could hurt her any more than she was already hurting.

"I'm sorry I wasn't honest with you sooner. And I—I mean what I said in that letter. I don't... I don't regret meeting you. But I... I think you know we've reached the end of the road. I think we both know we've reached the end of the road now. Right?"

Jonno looked up at her. His face was sodden with tears. He looked a broken man. A weak man. And if she didn't feel anything for him now, she might've felt sorry for him. For the man she thought he was. The man he used to be.

She braced herself, then said the words she'd wanted to say for months.

"It's... it's time for me to leave," she said.

Jonno put his head in his hands. Shook his head. Muttered something under his breath.

And while he was in this state, while she had a chance that she might not get again, Tara turned around.

Walked towards the stairs.

She'd grab a rucksack she'd already packed with enough to get her by for a couple of days, and then she'd go.

She didn't want to come back here.

She just wanted to get back to her parents.

She just wanted to start again.

She had just about reached the bottom step when she felt something.

A sharp pain, right on the back of her head.

Her hair being yanked back.

Her neck jolting.

And then she felt herself being dragged to the floor.

Slamming against it.

She didn't understand. What'd happened? Jonno had never been physically violent. And he wouldn't be. So what...

She turned around and looked up and saw him crouching over her.

He grabbed her by the throat.

Tightened his grip around her neck.

And he started into her eyes with wide, bloodshot eyes.

"You're not going anywhere," he said.

She was too terrified to notice every single light in the house flicker off.

CHAPTER NINE

When the lights went out in the vets, Sam had no idea of the significance right now.

Nobody did.

But he was very close to finding out.

The vets' reception area went dark. A few miserable, lifeless customers screamed, and the dogs started barking and howling even louder.

And in front of him, on that reception desk, he heard the snotty receptionist who was bizarrely in the midst of reporting him to the police.

"Hello? Are—are you still there? Is anyone there?"

Sam smiled. A power cut. A serious bloody power cut, right in the midst of this arsehole receptionist reporting him to the police.

He looked up at the ceiling. Right up into the darkness.

"Whoever's up there looking over me... thank you."

And then he looked back down.

People were scurrying over to the vets' windows, peering out at that torrential rain. Some of them were pointing out at something, getting carried away by something. A crash or something. Sam wasn't sure. He wasn't listening very closely.

Because right now, he only had one focus.

One goal.

He was going to get Harvey out of here.

And nobody was going to stop him.

He walked across the waiting room towards the first door on the left, where he knew Harvey would be waiting for him because he'd been in there with him before. Hurt his paw when he was a pup. And the poor sod was terrified of the vets back then. Shook like a leaf as Sam held onto him while they injected some painkillers.

He remembered holding on to him and hearing Harvey's heavy panting and telling him everything would be okay.

And even though he was making that promise to Harvey... he was making it to himself, too.

Because that wasn't long after he'd lost Rebecca.

After he'd left the military, once and for all.

After he left those awful memories behind him.

He kept on walking towards the door where the vets would be, and he noticed an old couple by his side. They were both struggling with their phones in the darkness.

"I told you, Sheila," the man said. "It's not switching on."

"You're not the only one," another man said. "My phone's dead as they come."

And then he heard another voice. One of the vets, running out of the side rooms, panic in his eyes. "Even the backup generator's down. No idea what's going on."

Sam had to admit that was weird. Either nobody here paid much attention to their battery, or something weird had happened. But it was probably just a coincidence. There was no way a power cut could wipe out phones, too. Absolutely impossible.

And backup generators as well?

All at once?

A coincidence. Surely a coincidence.

Unless…

No.

The odds of an EMP attack or some kind of CME solar event were minuscule.

Even though he'd spent years preparing for the eventuality of disaster… it still felt like the *reality* of disaster was far from possible.

He thought about the logistics of an electromagnetic pulse. Or a coronal mass ejection. The devastation both would cause.

And if there was one on the horizon, people would be warned.

Right?

He shook his head. He was getting carried away. And he was getting distracted.

He needed to find Harvey.

He needed to get him out of here.

And then he needed to get that battery for his car and get back home.

The sooner he got out of the city, the better.

He was pretty much done with this place at this point.

He rushed closer towards that door, closer towards Harvey, when suddenly someone appeared right in front of him.

It was the woman. The receptionist.

Standing there.

Blocking the door with her arms.

"You—you aren't authorised to take another step beyond this door, sir."

Sam shook his head. "You really are a piece of work, aren't you?"

He tried to push around her.

But she stepped to the right, blocking his way even more.

"I'm not messing around, sir," she said. "You are not entering this room. You are not leaving this place with your dog."

Sam felt anger.

Rage towards this woman for what she was implying.

He'd never hurt Harvey.

Harvey had saved his life.

He'd saved his life when he was at his lowest ebb. And whatever this woman's problem was, wherever it came from... he wasn't having anyone accusing him of being a monster.

Especially not where his dog was concerned.

"I'm here for my dog," Sam said. "I'll settle the bill with you. Hell, I'll pay double if it gets you off my case."

"I don't think you understand—"

"No," Sam said, taking a further step forward. "I don't think *you* understand. You're going to move out of my way. Or I'll move you my goddamned self."

"Is that a threat?"

Sam shook his head. "Take it however you want."

He waited for the woman to move.

Waited for her to step aside.

But she wasn't moving.

She wasn't budging at all.

Behind him, he heard more complaining about dead phones. He heard a few shouts by the window, but most of them were drowned out by the sound of the torrential rain.

He heard all this weird panic and confusion, and it took him back.

It sparked a memory in his mind.

The heat.

The dryness in his throat.

The brightness of the desert sun.

Don't go! Please! Don't—don't leave me!

The shouting.

The screaming.

He closed his burning eyes.

No. Not now. No.

He opened his eyes.

The receptionist stood there in front of the room.

Smirking.

"Are you ready to follow your orders now?" she said.

Follow your orders, Sam. Follow your goddamned—

No!

Don't think about that.

Don't think about—

"Or are we going to have a problem here?"

Sam looked into this woman's eyes, and he shook his head.

"I don't know what your problem is with me. But I..."

It all happened so fast, then.

Behind him, he heard screaming.

"Plane!" someone cried. "Fucking plane!"

And then he saw the look on the receptionist's face.

The way she went pale.

The way her face started glowing orange.

"What..." she started.

Dread started to build inside Sam.

What the hell?

He turned around.

Looked over at the front window.

He didn't have long to process what he was looking at.

But when he saw it, he couldn't think about anything else.

There was a plane hurtling through the sky.

Burning through the dark grey cloud.

Flying right towards the vets.

Terrified customers ran past him, scrambling to get past him, to get through the doors, to get into the back of the vets, to get away from here.

Dogs barked.

Cats meowed.

People screamed.

"What..." he muttered.

He didn't have time to say anything else.

He grabbed the receptionist and dragged her down to the floor, behind the counter.

And the next thing he heard was the enormous explosion.

A burst of heat blasted through the reception area, carrying with it a cascade of screams.

And then, darkness.

Total darkness.

CHAPTER TEN

Tara felt Jonno's hands tightening around her throat, and she started to wonder if this was how it ended.
Dead, at the hands of the man who'd just proposed to her.
Dead, at the hands of a man she should've walked away from a long, long time ago.
Dead.
Jonno gripped her throat with both hands now. He stared down at her with bloodshot, tearful eyes. Specks of saliva dangled from his chin. He looked deranged. Like a rabid animal.
Tara's throat hurt like mad. And as much as Tara never liked feeling like a shrinking violet because that just never was her, she felt terrified right now. She couldn't breathe. She couldn't breathe, her vision was fading, and she was going to pass out and die.
This was all her life was going to amount to.
Dead at the hands of the man everyone warned her about.
All because she'd been too stupid to see the red flags.
Or too naive to want to see them.
Or kidding herself about just how strong and independent she really was...

She grabbed Jonno's hands. Tried to pull them away, digging her nails into his skin. "P... Pl..."

Jonno tightened his grip. Leaned right into her face. "You don't get to just walk away. You don't get to write a letter like that and then just walk away, you selfish bitch. That's your problem. Selfish. And you always have been selfish. But that ends. That all ends, right here."

The pain in Tara's neck grew worse. Fear intensified. She was going to die. She was going to die, and there was nothing she could do about it.

She dug her nails into the backs of Jonno's hands even harder because it was about the only thing she could do right now.

"Pl..." she gasped. "Plea..."

Jonno smirked. His eyes that used to look at her so softly and with so much love looked at her with hatred right now. Like he was enjoying seeing her in this way. Like he loved the power he had over her. "I'll tell you what's going to happen. You're going to stay here. We're going to ride out this storm together. And I'm going to teach you a lesson or two about what happens when you step out of line. Okay? That's what happens here."

Tara shook her head. Kept on digging her nails in.

"You're pathetic," Jonno said. "A pathetic, weak, ugly little bitch. I used to love you. Really, I did. And maybe I will love you again. But you've got a lot of changing to do to get to that point. A *lot* of changing."

She felt intense sadness. Because as horrible as the things he'd said to her over the years were... this physical violence was new. It was unprecedented. It was something she'd never experienced from him before.

And she felt so weak. So pathetic. Because this wasn't *her*. She wasn't the sort of woman who ended up in this kind of situation. She was strong. She'd always been strong. She did things her way; she didn't take any shit.

And that just made her feel even more ashamed.

Ashamed of how far she'd fallen.

Ashamed that she'd ended up in a position where she felt like she couldn't even fight.

Because that was just not her.

Jonno leaned in closer to her face. His hands were still tight around her throat. Her vision was fading. Her breathing was getting harder and harder. Her body was shaking, her hands were going weak, and she couldn't dig her nails into him much longer.

"You're going to get up. You're going to go to the bathroom, and you're going to get yourself cleaned up. And then you're going to come back in here, and we're going to put all this behind us, and we're going to watch a nice fucking movie. Because I'm not having you ruining my night or my weekend. I've had a stressful enough week at work as it is. Understand?"

Tara's vision faded. She could barely move a muscle.

"I said, do you *understand*?"

Tara nodded.

She hated that she nodded.

Because it made her feel even more subservient.

Even weaker.

"Good," Jonno said. "I'm glad."

And then he loosened his grip.

Tara gasped a lungful of air. She rolled over onto her side and spluttered thick saliva, bile, and a little blood onto the carpet.

"No," Jonno said. "No, no, no, you messy bitch. What the hell?"

He grabbed her hair.

Yanked her head back.

Pain split through her neck.

"Jonno—"

"You don't do *that* on my carpet, you animal," he shouted. "You absolute dirty little animal. No way."

Tara felt anger rising inside her body.

She felt something shift inside her.

The weeks, months, and years of his belittling comments.

Of him shrinking her world.

And now the violence.

The way he was speaking to her.

The things he was saying to her.

The way he was making her feel.

"You need teaching a lesson or two," Jonno said, yanking her hair further back.

Tara saw the wine bottle on the table beside the sofa, right in front of her.

"No," she said.

"What was that?"

Tara didn't think.

She just grabbed the bottle of red wine, two-thirds full.

"This is my fucking carpet," she said. "I paid for it. And I'll do whatever I fucking want on it."

And then she swung that wine bottle back.

Across his face.

Hard.

She heard it smash.

Felt Jonno's grip on her loosen.

Felt lukewarm wine spill all over her.

The smell of alcohol filled the air.

And then she heard a thud.

She crouched there. Crouched there on the floor, heart racing. Taking in deep breaths. In through the nostrils, out through the mouth. In through the nostrils, out through the mouth.

She didn't want to look back.

She didn't want to look at the room.

She didn't want to see.

But she couldn't hide from the truth forever.

The truth of what she'd done.

She turned around.

Slowly.

The cream carpet she'd spent so much of her savings on was covered in red wine.

Sharp, broken shards of dark glass pointed up from the floor.

And lying in the middle of the floor, Jonno.

Lying there, eyes closed.

He looked peaceful. Like he could be sleeping.

But then she saw the blood trickling from his head.

From the corners of his lips.

Staining the carpet a different shade of red.

Completely still.

CHAPTER ELEVEN

When Sam opened his eyes, he was convinced he was in Hell.

All around him, he could hear screaming. Wailing. People crying out at the top of their lungs in absolute agony. He could smell smoke. Charred flesh, so strong in the air and thick in his lungs, it made him gag. He could taste blood on his lips, and his body felt hot—and it was getting hotter and hotter. There was someone on top of him. Something pressing down on his chest, squeezing the air from his lungs.

He blinked a few times and looked around.

He was in the vets. The waiting room at the vets. His memories were blurry. He'd come in here drenched because his car broke down. Some stroppy cow wouldn't let him get to his Harvey.

And then...

Something happened.

He remembered the screaming.

Remembered people running past him.

Remembered turning around and seeing it hurtling towards the windows, burning through the grey skies.

A plane.

An airplane, of all fucking things.

Hurtling towards them.

He coughed. Tried to move, tried to stand. But there was something on top of him. Something heavy pinning him down to the floor. He blinked a few times, looked around, and he saw other people lying there. Ducking down. Hiding.

And then, when he blinked, he realised they weren't hiding.

They were lying still.

Blood underneath them.

Dead.

He saw dogs running past, jumping over the flames of this wreckage. He saw a couple of pups sitting right beside their owners, whining, wagging their tails nervously as they waited for their humans to wake up.

And then, by his side, he heard something.

Spluttering.

Coughing.

He turned around.

There was a woman beside him. Her face was covered in cuts and bruises. Her body was covered in blood.

And for a second, as he stared at this woman, he was back in Iraq.

Please help us. Please!

He was right there again, and this was a waking nightmare, and it was all happening, all over again.

And then he blinked, and he looked at this woman, and he realised it wasn't the woman from Iraq at all.

He wasn't back there.

It was the receptionist.

The one who'd been arsey with him.

The one blocking him from getting to Harvey.

He didn't like the woman. Didn't like her one bit for suggesting he was failing Harvey's welfare in some way.

But seeing her like this…

Blood pouring down her face.

Crying.

Terrified.

And blood trickling from her lips, too.

She was human.

And whatever reasons she'd had for wanting to keep him away from Harvey, he had to put that to one side right now.

He had to…

Harvey.

Shit.

Harvey.

He looked around.

Looked at the door to his left.

The door he knew his dog would be behind.

And then he looked back at the receptionist.

Flames flickering so close, making his skin all hot.

Smoke filling his lungs and making him dizzier and dizzier.

He strained to push the heavy chunk of metal from him. Plane debris. It was heavy, and it was hard to move.

He strained with all the strength he had.

But it was just too heavy.

It was pinning him down too hard.

And those flames definitely weren't getting any further away.

He looked around at the woman. The receptionist, sitting there, bleeding out. She had her hand over her chest. Blood was pouring out, through her fingers, down her hand, dripping to the floor. Shit. She was in a bad way. A really bad way.

Sam swallowed a lump in his dry throat. "You hold on, okay? Just… just hold on."

The huge chunk of debris pressed right down on him. It felt like it had a life and a strength of its own.

Sam took as deep a breath as he could, which sent a sharp pain right down his back.

He gritted his teeth.

He was getting out of this.

He had to.

He pushed.

Pushed as hard as he could.

He felt the debris lifting slightly.

His muscles were on fire.

And the screams...

The gargled cries of the dying...

He pushed harder against that debris.

Up ahead, he heard something crash against the floor.

Something from the vets' roof.

This place was falling apart.

He needed to get out of here.

Right fucking now.

He gritted his teeth again. Shaking. Weak. And fully aware that if he didn't get out of this mess as soon as possible, he was going to be crushed, impaled, or burned alive.

He didn't fancy any of those options.

"Come on, Sam. Come on. If not for yourself... for Harvey."

He closed his eyes.

He held his breath.

He zoned out of the screams and the intense heat getting closer, the suffocating smoke filling his lungs, and the blood on his lips, and he pushed.

The debris shifted.

Shifted just enough that he could breathe again.

And then he dragged himself out of it.

"That's it. That's—"

The debris creaked and shifted, started sliding down towards Sam's legs.

He dragged his legs out of the way.

Tumbled back.

The debris fell and hit the floor.

Right where he'd lay trapped just moments ago.

Sam stared at that spot. Stared at the large metal chunk of debris and how close it was to snapping his legs in two.

He was lucky to be alive.

Used at least two of his nine lives today already, that was for sure.

And then he heard the whimper.

He turned around.

The receptionist.

Holding her blood-drenched torso with her hand.

Sam limped over to her.

Crouched right in front of her. "Hey," he said. "We're—we're gonna be okay. We're gonna get you out of..."

And then he saw it.

The chunk of metal.

Right through her chest.

Piercing right through her body.

He looked up into her eyes.

She looked back at him, just at the wrong time.

He saw the tears in her watery eyes.

He saw the horror on her face.

Her skin so pale.

Where it wasn't smeared with blood, anyway.

He wanted to comfort her. He wanted to reassure her.

He didn't want her to die on him.

And then the receptionist reached out.

She grabbed Sam's hand.

Tight.

"Please," she begged. "I... Help me. Please—please help me."

Sam looked into this woman's desperate eyes as she clutched his hand for dear life, and he felt his whole world crumbling around him.

He felt like he was in a nightmare.

"Don't—don't leave me," the receptionist said. "Please don't... please don't..."

And all Sam could do was hold her shaking hand as her grip weakened.

All he could do was crouch there as the flames filled the vets.

As the screaming grew less and less frequent.

As the writhing bodies grew still.

"Don't leave me," the woman gasped, smoke making her voice crack and break up. "Don't..."

He held her hand until it went still.

Until the life drifted from her body.

Until she died in front of him.

He looked up at her.

Looked at the blankness in her eyes.

The emptiness.

"I'm sorry," he said. "I'm sorry... I'm sorry I couldn't do more."

And then he stood up.

Looked around at the flames.

Looked around at the bodies.

And looked around at the masses of blood, the chunks of flesh, and the severed limbs.

He looked at it all, and he wondered why he was still here.

Why he was always still here.

And then he turned around to that door he'd been trying to get through, to find Harvey, and to get the hell out of here.

"I'm coming for you, Harvey," he said. "I'm... I'm coming."

He staggered towards that door.

The vacant eyes of the dead receptionist stared up at him.

And the vacant eyes, back in Iraq, stared down on him, too.

Judging his every move.

CHAPTER TWELVE

Tara stared at Jonno's body lying on the living room floor, and she had no idea whether he was alive or dead.

The beige carpet was covered in two shades of red.

Red from the wine bottle, which she'd cracked over his head in a moment of pure anger, a moment of sheer rage. A moment that all these years of being degraded and treated like shit had built towards.

And then red blood.

Blood from his head. And quite a lot of it, too. A puddle of it, seeping right into the carpet.

He was bleeding from his mouth, too. His eyes were closed and totally still. He hadn't moved an inch since she'd hit him.

And she knew what that meant.

A crippling sense of fear stormed through her body. She felt sick, her stomach tensing up. She wanted to puke. She'd killed him. She was a fucking killer.

And even if he *wasn't* dead…

She was in the shit.

Fuck.

She was in so much shit.

She was going to go to prison.

She was going to get out of prison one day, and either she'd have absolutely nothing left, *or* he'd still be alive, and he'd still be waiting for her, and she'd be more reliant on him than ever before, and...

She closed her eyes.

Took a deep breath.

Breathe, Tara. Breathe.

She opened her eyes.

Saw Jonno lying there right before her.

And that fear hit her again, just as fresh as before.

She crippled over. Clutched her stomach. She wasn't weak. She was strong. She always had been strong.

And he'd put her through hell.

He'd been psychologically torturing her for years.

But...

Two things.

First the guilt.

The guilt over what she'd done.

The guilt that always returned.

And then the realisation that this was the man she'd loved more than any man in her entire life...

Only...

No.

Even *that* she felt guilty about.

Because Jonno was a monster.

Her love for this man was long gone.

She felt no guilt over what she'd done.

She couldn't afford to feel any guilt.

She couldn't let herself suffer any more than she already had.

She looked up, then.

The door to the lounge right there.

Leading to the stairs.

Which led outside.

Out into the torrential rain.

She pictured it in her mind. Visualised running over there, through that door, down the stairs, and out into the rain.

She pictured walking through the water while everyone else tried to scramble back inside, and she pictured herself smiling.

She pictured being free.

But she couldn't.

She couldn't just run.

Could she?

She reached into her pocket for her phone, something that sent a shiver down her spine. Whenever she raised her phone, Jonno always wanted to know what she was looking at. And then he stopped asking, and she was pretty sure it's because he was tracking her somehow, monitoring her activity.

She looked at the screen, and something weird struck her.

It was dead.

Strange. She'd charged it just this afternoon. Made sure she had a full battery for her trip back to her parents' place.

Maybe it'd got damaged when the wine had spilled everywhere. Only... she didn't think so.

And it didn't look cracked or anything, either.

It was odd.

But then, stranger things had happened.

She heard thunder erupt outside. Saw lightning flash. Somewhere in the distance, she heard shouting in the street. Sounded like someone out there was really struggling in the storm.

And she felt lost. Lost in a haze. Lost in a dream.

Her phone was out.

Which meant she couldn't call the police.

She couldn't turn herself in, even if she wanted to.

And here she was.

Standing over Jonno's body.

Heart racing.

And wondering.

What if?

She looked up at that door again, and suddenly it hit her.

In a moment of sheer spontaneity, in a moment that required no thought, and in a moment of deep, deep panic, Tara turned around and ran up the stairs.

She went into the bedroom.

Grabbed the rucksack she'd packed from underneath the bed.

And then she turned around and went to leave the bedroom.

She saw the photograph of her and Jonno on their bedside table, and she stopped.

Turkey. Three years ago. Smiles on both their faces. Right after they'd been paragliding.

She looked at the smile on her face and the smile on his face, and she wondered at what moment things went so, so horribly wrong for them.

And then she turned around.

She ran down the stairs.

Back into the lounge.

She stopped.

Stopped when she saw Jonno again.

Lying there.

Eyes still closed.

Fingers curled in an unnatural position.

Even more of that blood staining the carpet that Tara had paid for.

The smell of spilled red wine strong in the air.

She wanted to go over to him. To wake him up. To apologise.

She wanted to use this moment to start again.

To show him what happened when he pushed her too far.

To make him apologise and for them to go back to the good days.

But as she stood there, she realised that was a fantasy.

It was a total fantasy.

And in that dreamlike haze, Tara knew she only had one choice right now.

She looked down at Jonno's body and wiped the tears from her eyes.

She should call the police.

She should turn herself in.

She should ring an ambulance and get him seen to.

But then she heard a rival voice in her head.

A louder voice.

A voice she knew she shouldn't listen to.

But a voice she couldn't resist.

Go.

Get out of here.

Run.

She listened to that voice.

And as much as she knew it was the wrong road to go down, as much as she knew how much deep, deep shit it would get her into... she wasn't being controlled by Jonno any longer.

She wasn't going out on his terms.

She was having her moment of freedom.

However brief that moment may be.

She stood there in the living room.

And then she stepped over Jonno's body, through the lounge door, down the stairs, and out into the torrential rain.

She didn't look back once.

Tara knew she was running towards a very different life.

She just had no idea quite how different that life was going to be yet.

CHAPTER THIRTEEN

Sam pushed open the door to one of the surgery rooms in the vets, and he had a horrible feeling he was going to find Harvey's dead body lying there waiting for him.

The smoke was thick, and it was really getting on his chest and making him feel dizzy. What remained of the waiting area behind him was completely destroyed and wrecked, and he could feel the heat radiating behind him from the flames. He couldn't hear any struggling anymore. No whining. No struggling. No fighting for life.

And that was chilling.

The sound of people struggling for dear life was awful. The worst thing in the world.

But when the silence came in its place...

That was even more horrifying.

He thought about the woman. The receptionist. Clinging to his hand with her shaking fingers.

Please don't leave me...

Please...

And that sense of defeat.

That sense that he hadn't been able to do a thing about it to help her.

He lifted his head.

He needed to get Harvey.

And he needed to get out of here.

There was nothing else he could do.

The surgery room looked in remarkably decent shape. The windows at the back were intact. The metal table in the middle of the room stood tall. It looked like the worst of the crash had affected the waiting area at the front of the building.

And that was a relief. That was a major fucking relief.

Only one problem.

There was no sign of Harvey.

Sam looked around the room.

He looked under the table.

He looked over at the computer system at the back of the room.

At the frosted windows, heavy rain banging against them.

But there was nowhere to hide in here.

There was no sign of Harvey here.

He was gone.

He turned around to that side door. The one patients weren't meant to go through. The one that led back to one of the other surgery areas.

Visions plagued his mind.

The thought of finding Harvey's dead body.

The pain that would cause him.

A pain unlike any he'd ever experienced.

And then he tightened his fists.

Shook his head.

"Whatever you find," he said. "You're gonna have to take a look, Sam. No point standing here and wasting time."

He walked over to the door.

Grabbed the handle.

Held his breath.

Come on. You know what you have to do.

He counted down a few seconds.

And then he lowered that handle.

Pushed the door open.

The lights in this room were out, like the rest of the lights in this place. He could smell a medicinal stench in the air and the unmistakable aroma of urine. There were no windows in this back bit of the vets, so it was dark in here. As dark as night.

But as Sam stood there, he soon realised this area of the vets hadn't got away quite as unscathed.

Water was pouring through a hole in the roof from the cloudy, stormy skies above.

There was debris all over the floor. Large chunks of concrete and metal.

And lying there on the floor, there was a woman dressed in blue.

Sam recognised her right away. Emma, she was called. Blonde hair. Short. Always such a pleasant girl. Harvey loved her—as much as any dog loved a vet, anyway. Some of the vets didn't get Harvey. Said he was snappy and weren't keen. But Emma always had a special bond with Harvey. And that counted for a lot. A hell of a lot. Only damned reason he persisted with this place, in all truth.

And seeing her here right now, he found it hard to believe Emma would ever raise any welfare concerns about Harvey. He knew for a fact it wasn't the sort of thing she'd do. It was reception. Middle-management. It always was, wasn't it?

Either way, Sam would never get a chance to ask.

Because Emma was quite clearly dead.

There was a big nasty gash on her head, which blood pooled out of. Her skull looked cracked like an Easter egg. Those pretty blue eyes stared up into the darkness, almost like they were shocked.

And seeing her like this... it sparked that sense of dread inside Sam again.

The memories.

The memories of the horror in his past.

The memories of Iraq.

The memories of...

He closed his eyes.

Shook his head.

And then he opened his eyes and looked back up, across this room, and into the darkness.

The room was silent but for that pouring rain waterfalling down from above. Or maybe it wasn't. Maybe the sound of that falling rain was masking everything else. His ears *were* ringing pretty badly since the crash, too. He wasn't sure.

He looked around, into the darkness. Looked at the operating table before him, which was thankfully empty of any animals.

He looked at the pictures of happy dogs on the walls all around him.

And then he heard it.

Barking.

Barking from the room to the left.

And not just one dog barking.

Lots of dogs.

All of them barking.

A knot in his stomach. Of course. There'd be dogs in there. Dogs who'd been operated on. Dogs who were waiting for their owners to pick them up. Shit. The worry those owners would go through when they got here. The panic they'd experience, seeing the state of this building.

And then the relief that the area where the dogs were recovering was all okay. All intact.

The animals were fine.

And then there was Harvey.

He rushed over to that door, over the pools of water, over the sharp chunks of debris.

He opened that door right up.

And what he saw broke his heart.

Dogs.

Dogs in cages.

All of them were right up at the front of the cages, barking, howling, eager to get out, eager to escape.

And in that back corner... he saw something that made his heart skip a beat.

"Harvey," he said.

Harvey looked right at him. His ears went back. He started wagging his tail, then barking.

And Sam couldn't contain his delight.

He couldn't contain his relief.

He couldn't mask how damned happy he was to see his pup right now.

He ran across the room, past the barking dogs, towards Harvey. "Harvey," he said. "Good lad. It's okay. Don't worry. Don't you worry at all. I'm here, alright? I'm here."

Harvey barked back at him, wagging his tail. Clearly very damned eager to get out of this cage.

Sam crouched down, started to turn the lock. "Welfare concerns. Frigging welfare concerns. And they have you locked in a cage. What the hell's with that, hmm?"

Harvey barked back at him like he was acknowledging what he was saying.

Sam struggled with the lock. Twisted it open with his shaking fingers.

"Almost there," he said. "Almost..."

The lock sprung open.

The metal doors swung open.

And Harvey launched himself at Sam, knocking him right back to his arse.

"Harvey," Sam said, laughing, trying to stop Harvey licking his face. "That's—I know, lad. I know. I'm pleased to see you too. Just not... just not in front of everyone like this, huh? Now's not the time or the place."

Harvey didn't seem to be listening. He continued to lick Sam's face relentlessly.

Sam stroked Harvey back, gently wrestling his weight from his body. Not that he didn't *want* to be attacked by Harvey's slobber or bathed in affection right now. He bloody loved it. He was so happy to find Harvey. He didn't know what he'd do without him. How he'd get by. How he'd cope.

But as nice as it was to get such a greeting... he knew there were serious matters at hand right now.

Like getting the hell out of this place.

He pushed Harvey away gently and got back to his feet. And then it struck him that it *was* weird that there were no sirens outside. No police or fire brigades or ambulances—that he could hear, anyway. He was in the middle of the city. An incident like this wouldn't go unnoticed, especially not with a police station nearby.

The lights.

The phones.

The backup generators.

The plane.

And the... silence.

Something wasn't right. It didn't take a genius to see that much.

And he had a sickening feeling in his chest that he might know what was going on here.

Exactly what was going on here.

He looked at the door in front of him. Frosted glass. He knew it'd lead out into a little run area, where they let dogs have a wee and a little play when they'd been operated on or seen to. He could get out that way. And then he could get a battery for his car and get back home.

Which seemed insane, really. He knew what Rebecca would've said. *You need to get yourself to the hospital. You could have a bleed.* She always thought he was stubborn. And she was probably right—not that he ever admitted that publicly.

But no. As achy as he felt and as much as the taste of blood on his lips was unpleasant, the best thing for him and Harvey right now was to get back home.

If he felt rough in a few days, he could get the doctors involved then.

"Come on, lad. Let's…"

And then he heard the barking behind him.

He turned around.

All those other dogs, standing at the front of their cages, barking like mad.

A golden Labrador puppy.

A grumpy-looking border terrier.

A westie, characteristically yappy.

He looked at all these dogs, and he knew he couldn't just leave them here. Sure, it wasn't his place to set them free. Some of them could do a runner and go missing, and their owners would definitely *not* appreciate that.

But at the same time… this building was on fire. There was no telling what might happen next or how much worse it would get.

He needed to let them out.

Get them outside.

Find someone—police, fire service, anyone—who could help take them in.

It might mean some of them got away and never saw their owners again.

But if their owners knew it meant their survival, then surely they'd approve.

He swallowed a lump in his throat.

"Come on, you yappy lot. Let's get you out of here."

He walked down the room and unlocked the crates, one by one.

And as these dogs all jumped out, one by one, he felt like the fucking pied piper.

"Alright," he said. "Alright. Less of that nonsense. Come on. Orderly queue, the lot of you. Let's get out of here."

He stood there, surrounded by dogs, and he looked back at this building. He looked at the rain pouring in through the torn roof. He smelled the smoke and the burning flesh. He felt the heat from the flames. And he couldn't believe it. Couldn't believe he was still standing. Couldn't believe that he was the last one left.

He gulped.

Gritted his teeth.

And then he turned around to that back door and stepped outside.

Into the unknown.

CHAPTER FOURTEEN

Tara waded down the waterlogged street as quickly as she could and tried to get the thought that she was a murderer out of her head.

The weather was bad. Really bad. If it looked bad inside, then it was even worse out in it. She was absolutely drenched to the bone. Her clothes were completely sodden. The rucksack on her shoulders, where she'd stuffed enough clothes to get by wearing—and a few other sentimental things—was almost certainly drenched through. And the water on the pavements was bad. It was like trekking through a stream.

Or more like a *river*.

And the scariest thing?

It didn't look like it was getting any better or easing off.

She saw a few cars in the middle of the road beside her. People were sitting in them. The first one on her left—this grey Vauxhall Astra—had a family inside it. Husband at the wheel. He was holding his phone. Looked like he was trying to use it, but kept on slamming his finger against it, like he was struggling to get it working. He looked pissed off. Really pissed off. And his wife had her head in her hands.

They were stuck in the water. In the middle of the road. That was bound to be frustrating. Really fucking frustrating.

But it was that phone that caught Tara's eye.

The way the pair in the front of the car were holding up their phones now, showing them to one another.

Showing those black screens to each other.

And she thought of her own phone.

How it'd lost charge already, something she found hard to believe.

She didn't understand it. Couldn't explain it.

But there had to be a reason for it.

And she wondered if there could be a link, somehow.

But how?

No severe weather would wipe out phones like this, right?

Unless there'd been some sort of weird power surge while her phone was plugged in. But then she didn't think so. She was pretty sure the phone was working when she'd unplugged it.

She turned, kept her head down, and walked further down the road. The rain seemed to fall heavier, which Tara found very hard to believe. Her hair was absolutely drenched and stuck to her face. She could taste it, cold against her lips.

And every step she took through this deep water, she kept on remembering what'd happened back at the house.

What she'd done back at the house.

She thought of Jonno, lying there in a pool of his own blood and wine.

And she couldn't actually believe she'd just walked away from him. Left him there. What the hell was she thinking?

But she was already walking. And nothing seemed to be stopping her. Like she was on autopilot, and she wasn't in control of her actions anymore.

She'd already attacked him.

Killed him.

Or left him for dead.

And she'd already run away.

If she went back there, and he was dead, she was in deep shit. She was going to jail. She was finished. No matter what sob story she tried to spin.

And if he was alive…

A feeling of dread in her chest.

A feeling of dread that felt even worse than the thought he might be dead.

If he was alive and she went back there…

She remembered how he'd pinned her down.

Choked her.

She remembered the violence in his eyes.

The feeling that he could kill her.

That at that moment, he was physically capable of taking her life.

She remembered the fear she'd felt, and she worried that if she went back there and he was alive… she was sentencing herself to death.

No.

No, she needed to get to her parents' place.

She needed to get a bus to the train station.

And *then* when she was there… when she was safe and away from him… that's when she'd call the police.

That was the right thing to do. She could say she was terrified. That she'd acted in self-defence. That she'd been left with no choice.

Which was true, right?

Fuck. She hated how weak she sounded in her own head.

Jonno was a monster.

And as horrible as it made her feel to admit it… he'd got what he deserved.

She was going to savour her final moments of freedom as she headed to her parents' place.

Whether the weather was terrible or not.

She dragged her feet through the cold, icy water. She couldn't stop shaking. She didn't know if she was just freezing cold with the rain, if it was the shock or a combination of both. Probably a combination of both.

She just needed to get to the bus stop. That was her first step. That was the first hurdle of her journey.

Get to the bus stop.

And then get to town.

And then... whatever happened after that, happened.

She saw more cars in the road. And it was weird. Because none of their engines seemed to be on. Up ahead, in the distance, she could see smoke. Flames? Fuck. Something must've happened. Had to be to do with the weather.

But it still felt... odd. It still didn't make sense.

She clutched her rucksack close to her back and saw the bus stop up ahead.

There was a bus right there.

Right at the stop.

She felt a sense of relief. Finally. A bit of luck. Usually, whenever she turned up at the bus stop, the bus would pull away the second she got there. She knew what the drivers were like. Definitely saw her in the mirror. Definitely pulled away on purpose. So she had to be on guard. She wasn't in the clear just yet.

She ran. Ran down the pavement. Cold rainwater splashing up at her. A sickening, nauseating sense of fear intensifying inside her.

But also a sense of freedom.

A horrible, guilt-inducing sense of freedom.

Jonno was gone.

The source of all her problems, worries, and misery was gone.

She allowed herself a moment without dread.

A moment without suffering.

A moment to feel *herself* again, just as she used to feel.

She ran up to the bus and reached the door.

"Single to town," she said, stepping onto the bus, completely drenched, dripping onto the floor.

The driver was a chubby man wearing a hi-vis jacket. He didn't look at Tara. He just shrugged. "Sorry. Not goin' anywhere."

Tara's stomach sank. Shit. "I... I just need to get to town. Really urgently."

The driver looked at her now. Narrowed his eyes. Like he didn't have time for this shit. "And I wanna get home, too. To my wife. To my kids. But I'm stuck out here with no power on the bus, staring at a bunch of cars who've just cut out, in the middle of the road, in the middle of a bloody storm."

Tara looked out the front window of the bus.

Saw more cars on the road.

None of their lights were on.

They were just stood there.

Stationary.

Dead.

"And just to make things worse, I can't even let my family know or listen to some bloody music to pass some time, because my shitty phone's decided *now's* the time to give up. Now, of all frigging times."

Tara looked around at the driver. "Your... your phone's gone too?"

The driver looked back at her. Scanned her, head to toe and back again. Nodded. "Anyway. You can shelter here for a bit if you want. I can't imagine I'll be going anywhere for a bit."

Tara stood there at the door of the bus.

Her hair plastered to her face.

Water dripping from her rucksack and her clothes.

And as she looked out at those stationary cars and then at that smoke rising in the distance... she couldn't stop thinking about the phones.

She didn't know what was happening.

But she knew one thing was for sure.

This was no ordinary storm.

She looked around at the driver, and she forced a smile. "It's... it's okay. I really... I really need to get to town."

The driver grunted. "Well, good luck to you. I'd lend you a canoe if I had one."

Tara stepped off the bus and back out into the rain.

She saw people in their homes opposite.

She saw them looking out the windows.

None of those houses were lit up.

She saw the cars.

No lights.

And she reached into her pocket again.

Pulled out her phone.

Dead.

She took a deep breath.

Put that phone back away.

And as she walked into the rain, reaching the train station still her goal, she couldn't deny that something was happening here.

Something very, very off.

CHAPTER FIFTEEN

Jonno opened his eyes.

His head hurt. Bad. His ears were ringing so loud it was actually painful to listen to. He could taste something rusty and metallic on his lips, and he knew it was blood.

But why could he taste blood?

Why was his head hurting so much?

The answer was on the tip of his tongue, and he just couldn't quite reach it.

He squinted around the room he was in. The lounge, by the looks of things. He was lying on his back. He could smell something... alcoholic. Something strong, so strong it was making his eyes water. Wine?

What had happened here?

He rolled onto his side and saw the red mess on the carpet. And then he saw something drip down from his head.

And when it dripped down, this red blob, and hit the carpet, he realised not all the red mess on the carpet was from the wine.

He was bleeding.

He reached up. Touched the back of his head. Felt something

sharp there. Searing pain burned through his skull. Fuck! He clenched his jaw and held his breath. Pulled his fingers away.

When he squinted at his fingers, he saw blood.

His stomach turned. He felt dizzy, and he felt sick. Something had happened. Something bad. He'd been attacked. Someone had attacked him and left him bleeding on the living room floor.

He needed to get up.

He needed to find Tara.

He...

His stomach dropped.

Everything froze.

Tara.

He remembered, then.

In an instant, he remembered everything.

The letter.

The argument.

Pinning her down.

And then the pain.

The pain against the back of his skull.

And now...

He dragged himself to his feet. Stood there, a little dizzy, a little wobbly, but standing.

He looked out the window. Saw the grey skies. Saw the torrential rain pouring down. Saw the stationary cars and the river of water washing down the road.

And then he turned around, and he looked at the door to the stairs.

It was half-open.

Ajar.

He saw it, and he felt anger creeping up inside him.

Embarrassment.

Betrayal.

He swallowed a bloody lump in his throat. And when he

couldn't swallow it completely, he spat it out onto the carpet—a shade of beige he'd always hated.

He wiped his mouth.

Clenched his fists.

And he took a deep breath.

Walked towards the door.

"I'll find you, Tara," he muttered. "I'll find you. And when I do… you'll regret this day for the rest of your fucking life."

CHAPTER SIXTEEN

It didn't take Sam long to realise something was wrong.
And it went way, way beyond a mere dose of "extreme weather."

The weather was bad, for sure. Make no mistake about it, this rain was torrential—and not torrential in the way old Brits usually say it is when they're sitting at a bus stop and complaining about a bit of drizzle. No, this was *properly* torrential. The roads were filled with water. The downpour didn't seem to be easing, either. If anything, it was getting worse.

But again, it wasn't the storm itself that was dominating Sam's thoughts right now.

He walked with Harvey by his side. He'd found a nice woman opposite the vets who promised to take the other dogs in and keep an eye on them until their owners showed up. *If* their owners showed up. And if not, she was animal crazy anyway, so Sam was very reassured she'd look after them.

And something she'd said had planted yet another seed in his head about what was happening here.

She said her telly wasn't working. Or her phones. Or anything at all in that house. Even her stairlift was knackered.

She said it was probably a power cut. Probably something to do with the storm. And that it would all be back online soon.

But Sam was starting to realise that wasn't the case.

The phones in the vets earlier. And the cars piled on the streets now.

Only one thing he could think of would bring society to a total standstill like this.

And it was far, far scarier than a mere power cut.

It was the result of an electromagnetic pulse—an EMP. Or a coronal mass ejection from the sun—a CME.

The mere thought that this might be what was going down made Sam's stomach turn. Sam had been researching solar storms for years. The biggest on record happened on Valentine's Day of 1859 and was known as the Carrington Event, after an astronomer called Richard Carrington. The event was unprecedented and completely bewildering. Auroras were seen as far down as Cuba, and apparently, people in many northern US states could read newspaper print from the glow of the lights alone.

But it wasn't all novelty. There were very serious consequences. The resulting geomagnetic disturbances caused sparks and fires from telegraph equipment and wreaked havoc across the US. Minor disturbances in the grand scheme of things, though.

But if the same thing happened today?

In today's interconnected, digital world?

Just imagine.

Technology governs every aspect of our lives. Even aspects of our lives we don't *think* it governs. Technology wakes us up. Technology keeps us warm. Technology feeds us, clothes us, and bathes us. Technology keeps our hearts beating at a perfect rate and keeps us breathing when we're unconscious.

In solar storms, a high-energy blast of sunlight ionises the Earth's atmosphere and wreaks havoc with radio communications.

And then, a deadly radiation storm, lethal to astronauts.

But it's the last stage that is so deadly.

The CME.

A cloud of particles drifting towards Earth and causing electromagnetic chaos.

GPS disruptions, destroying phones, airplanes, cars—and an entire trillion-dollar business.

Satellite communications completely essential to daily life. The meaning of money wiped out in an instant.

And then the electrical grid.

Power surges blowing out transformers. And these transformers aren't easy to replace overnight.

Especially if the power is so badly damaged that replacing them becomes nigh on impossible...

And the scary thing?

A coronal mass ejection from the sun is only one possibility. Solar storms are an inevitability. Humanity has just grown accustomed to burying their heads in the sand and pretending it won't happen, just like climate change and pandemics.

Burying their heads in the sand and hoping nothing will happen in their lifetime, and if it happens when they're dead, well, that's not their problem, is it?

But there are other possibilities, too. The possibilities for foreign powers to use nuclear weapons loaded with electromagnetic pulses in targeted attacks, causing the same outcomes as a CME, but in a more localised manner. A real prospect, growing ever more possible and being tested out in several conflicts across the globe in low-key, underreported fashions.

He looked around at the stationary cars.

At the people screaming at their phones, which were completely dead.

He looked at the people being carried through the streets, away from that plane wreckage, smeared in blood.

And then he looked down at his watch.

It wasn't only cracked now, which filled him with sadness

because he remembered how happy Rebecca was when she gave it him, how made up she knew he'd be by it.

But it'd stopped.

Stopped dead on four p.m.

That had to be around the time he'd stood in the vets.

About the time the lights went out.

Around the time the plane hurtled into the earth.

It could be a coincidence. It could be that he'd battered it hard enough that it'd killed it.

Or it could be something else.

An EMP or CME event.

He stood there and he knew things weren't going to go well in the city. He knew the situation here was going to deteriorate fast. Very fast. Because when the power collapsed, panic was going to set in. Looting was going to be rife. People were going to grow more and more desperate the longer and longer this progressed.

Especially when they saw things like planes falling from the skies…

Sam shuddered. For that to happen, it must be bad.

Really fucking bad.

The city was going to be in tatters.

And he wanted to be a long way from here when shit hit the fan even more than it already had.

Because if this was as wide scale as he thought it might be—as bad as it looked—then things would get worse before they got better.

Far, far worse.

And coupled with the storm…

Hell, this was a recipe for disaster.

He turned around.

Up ahead, he saw the high street. A place he really didn't want to go.

But he knew a store down there that he could grab some supplies from.

And also, that crucial battery, at another place a little further down. A guy he knew, Jeff. Ran a hardware store called Sparks. He could be useful.

His car was a long shot. An EMP would've fried any modern car, what with the computers built in nowadays.

But his car was probably just about old enough not to be affected.

Hopefully.

That was the plan, anyway.

"Come on, Harv," he said. "Let's... let's go get ourselves stocked up."

Sam walked through the water, away from the wreckage, and towards the high street.

He knew it was a risky move.

A move he might come to regret.

He just didn't realise quite how much this one, seemingly small decision was going to change the entire trajectory of his life.

Forever.

CHAPTER SEVENTEEN

Tara dragged her feet through the flowing water, and deep down, she knew she wasn't getting to the train station any time soon.

The streets were filled with cars. None of them were moving. And even weirder than that, none of them had any lights on. Very few engines were running at all.

People were sitting inside each of these cars. And as Tara walked past every single one of them, she saw the same thing, every time.

People holding their phones up.

Tapping at these jet-black screens.

The power completely gone.

Tara felt a knot tightening in her chest. She wasn't stupid. She was beginning to realise there was something seriously wrong going on here. And it didn't make sense that it was just some sort of issue with the electricity grid. It had to be worse than that. Because an issue with the electricity grid wouldn't wipe out phones. There had to be something else going on here.

Something even more serious.

Tara looked around at all these cars, all these people, stranded in the floods, stranded without power, and she knew that if things didn't resolve themselves soon, they would get pretty damned ugly, pretty damned fast.

She gritted her teeth. Saw the buildings of the inner city right up ahead. She didn't live far from the very centre, so in normal times she could probably make it there in around fifteen minutes.

But today was no normal day.

Either way, she knew she had to get there. She knew she had to keep going.

Get to her parents' place.

Get away from Jonno. From the memory of what she'd done to him. Of how she'd left him.

A bitter taste filled her mouth.

Don't think about that. Not right now.

What's done is done.

Get to your parents' place. And you can figure out the rest when you get there.

She took a deep breath, and she started walking again.

The water splashed against her thighs. The rain kept hurtling down from above. It definitely wasn't getting any lighter, that was for sure. If anything, it was getting heavier.

Tara knew about the weather warnings. But doesn't everyone just dismiss weather warnings, really? Usually, Britain's a very melodramatic place when it comes to weather forecasts and the like. A bit of snow was usually enough to bring public transportation to a standstill. So when talk of a bit of bad rain started spreading across the news, she hadn't really paid much attention to it.

And come to think of it... maybe there *was* mention that there could be power outages associated with the storms. But wasn't that just a typical warning?

And it still didn't explain why there was absolutely no power at all right now, as far as she could tell. Power cuts, she could understand. But the sort of blackout *this* seemed to be? How could anyone explain that?

She walked further through the water. Past more and more cars. Up ahead, she saw two blokes engaged in an argument about the position of a car. It looked like one guy's car *was* working—the first working car she'd seen—and he was struggling to get it out of the middle of the road. Right old banger, the car was. Which clearly pissed off the entitled bloke in the Tesla in front of him. Tesla man clearly couldn't understand why his fifty grand car wasn't budging while a rusty lump of metal was. In a way, it was quite funny.

She saw something else, then. An ambulance, with its back doors wide open. The two people in green uniforms were absolutely drenched—not just in rain but in tears. There was someone in the back. An old woman, by the looks of things. Lying completely still. Not moving a muscle. Not even twitching.

Tara's stomach sank. She knew these floods were dangerous in their own right. But coupled with whatever was happening with this power outage, it was goddamned lethal.

She turned around and focused on the road. The panic on the faces of the people in the cars. The dismay on the faces of those paramedics. And the memory that kept flashing into her mind.

Jonno.

Whacking that wine bottle over his head.

Knocking him to the floor.

Seeing his stationary body lying there, twitching.

A shiver shot up her spine.

She closed her eyes in the middle of the street.

You're going to be okay.

Whatever happens, you're going to be okay.

She thought about the emergency services then and the police. Or rather, the fact that she didn't see any coming to people's aid—because they couldn't, presumably. No police to keep society in order. No ambulances to help people. And surely fires would break out too. The longer this went on, the worse things were going to get.

She just had to hope the power came back on soon.

Even if... weirdly, the power being out benefited her.

It gave her a little more time before having to turn herself in.

For having to face up to her crimes.

She went to keep on walking, step by bloody step when suddenly she heard something right beside her.

It was someone gasping.

"Please... please... help..."

Tara turned around.

In the blue Honda Jazz beside her, she saw an old woman. She had short, curly hair. A flowery dress. She was probably in her eighties, but she looked really well for her age.

Only she was clutching her chest.

Gasping.

"Please... please..."

The hairs on the back of Tara's neck stood on end. She used to be a nurse once upon a time before Jonno made her quit her job because it was "clearly stressing her out"—and besides, he made enough money that the pair of them never needed to work again.

Tara loved her job as jobs went. Didn't realise it at the time, but when she quit, she really missed it. Missed the routine. Missed the sense of purpose it gave her.

When she tried to go back, Jonno always found some way to block or hinder her return. Just little things, like taking down the WiFi when she was submitting an application or "accidentally deleting" files she needed him to print.

It took a little while to realise exactly what he was doing and that all these "mistakes" weren't mistakes at all—they were a means of control.

And now, here she was. Penniless. Homeless, in a way, because Jonno's flat was Jonno's, and Jonno was... well, he was dead.

And if he wasn't dead, there was no way she was going back there.

But right now, her nurse's instincts kicked in.

This woman in front of her.

Gripping her chest.

Gasping for air.

Tara opened the car door and leaned over the woman. "Hey. I'm—I'm Tara. You're going to be okay, my love. I'm... I'm a nurse. I'm here to help you, okay?"

The woman coughed and spluttered. Saliva trickled down her chin. "Help. Please. Heart. My... Just like the last time. Please."

Tara couldn't fully follow the woman's broken speech. But she figured enough out from what she was saying to know she'd claimed she had a heart attack sometime in the past—and she was having one again now.

Tara cleared her throat. "I'm going to have to... Aspirin. Do you have any aspirin on you?"

The woman's eyelids closed and opened. She was drifting. She wasn't in a good way at all.

"Shit," Tara said.

She rushed over to the other side of the car, opened the door, and opened the glove compartment.

Papers tumbled out. A pack of mint imperials covered the floor like marbles.

But no aspirin.

"Aspirin," Tara shouted. "Does—does anyone have any aspirin around here?"

She looked around.

Looked at the people trapped in their cars, rain hammering down so heavily now that it shielded them from view.

"Anyone?" she shouted. "Does..."

She heard something that made all the hairs on her body stand on end.

A gasp. But one louder than she'd heard from this woman before.

A gasp like she'd heard back in the wards.

In intensive care.

And in palliative care.

A death gasp.

She looked around and saw the woman sitting there in her car.

Her eyes were open. The whites were on show. Her skin looked like it'd gone a shade greyer in a really short space of time. Her fingers were curled up in front of her, not flopping to the side like they might portray in the movies, but rigid.

And Tara didn't even need to check her pulse to know what this was.

"Shit," she said.

She ran over to her.

Did CPR on her.

Did chest compressions, and rescue breaths, trying to stay in the moment and totally stay in the zone.

"Come on," she said. "Please. Come on. Hang in there. You hang in there. Please."

She kept on going.

Kept on trying.

But time after time, no response.

She tried one final time, and then she fell back into the waterlogged road.

She sat there. Holding on to the woman's rigid hand. Stroking it slowly. A tear rolled down her cheek.

Because as the rain lashed down and as the panic began to grow even stronger on this road, she knew it was too late.

The woman was gone.

She saw a flash.

A flash of water.

A flash of dead eyes staring up at her.

A flash of lifelessness.

And then she pushed that flash away as quickly as she could.

She saw the woman lying dead before her, and her entire body went numb.

She was dead.

And she hadn't been able to save her.

CHAPTER EIGHTEEN

They say that if an electrical disaster strikes, there will be two waves of panic.

One driven by shock and desperation.

And the next driven by despair.

Of course, there'll be that initial shock. Think of it like a rollercoaster, where you suddenly plummet down a massive drop and think *that's* the main event, only to coast down a relatively straightforward bit of track after that.

Now that's like the first day or the first couple of days. That initial gut punch. That initial panic.

But still that sense of belief that things will get better.

That order will be restored.

Eventually.

Only then you hurtle down the next drop, which you realise is far bigger than the first.

And that drop just never stops falling.

Those are the days when realisation really begins to set in.

Those are the days the world changes.

Completely.

Think about it. That individual realisation everyone makes on their own that there's no power, and there's no news to tell them what to do, no police, no military, no order. At least not for a good while, anyway. But humanity's gut instinct is *supposedly* one of initial shock and paralysis. It's supposedly camaraderie and pulling together for a day or two. It's supposedly making the best of a bad situation, and "clapping for carers", and all that wholesome bullshit.

But right now, standing in the middle of the convenience store in the middle of the city centre, Sam realised humanity's downfall into disarray was far, far speedier than we liked to tell itself it would be.

It looked like people had skipped the camaraderie phase and were already sinking into disarray and lawlessness.

There were tons of people inside here, all of them scrambling for whatever they could stuff their trollies with. Presumably, the flood warnings had gone pretty much unnoticed—and it was only today realising just how bad those floods were, that people had started to take them seriously.

And they'd all decided to take it seriously all at once.

Coupled with the blackout... yeah, this did not make for a pleasant combination of circumstances right now.

The lights were all out in the supermarket, which made it intensely dark. You never realise just how unlit a supermarket is until you're standing in one with the lights off. You always assume they're these bright, luminous places until you realise all the light is completely artificial.

It was really dark in here. And that didn't help with the atmosphere of panic setting in.

Harvey growled by Sam's side.

Sam looked down at him. Sighed.

"Yeah," he said. "Me too. How about we get this done with as swift as possible, eh?"

Harvey barked back at him. Sam took that as a yes.

He grabbed a trolley, and he made straight for the aisles. He knew exactly what sort of things he needed—and mostly, he was just filling gaps because he had a fair few supplies stocked up for an emergency back at home anyway.

But there was a basic criterion: stuff with a long shelf life was crucial. Canned foods like chickpeas and lentils, high-protein foods like hard cheeses and peanut butter, and stuff like whole-wheat crackers too, which would last a long time; even if they did go soft, they didn't lose their nutritional value.

Easy storage was also important, making tins and cans just as useful. Shit like bacon, which people were naturally flocking to, was useless because it'd be off in a few days. It'd be both a waste of space and a waste in general. Farmers were sorted because they had their own living supplies of dairy. But without deliveries of supplies, even they were going to face serious challenges.

The list of ways in which the world was going to change really was endless.

Easily prepared meals were also important if there really was a widespread blackout. The sort of things you could cook over a portable stove, or even better, things that can be eaten as-is, without the need to heat if needed.

Nutritional value, calories, that sort of thing, they were all important. That's why peanut butter was an absolute miracle food, more than anything right now. High protein, nutritionally healthy, and high calories. The perfect food.

And yet so many people here in this store were ignoring it.

They were preparing for a few days of outages, when they should be thinking much, much longer than that.

As much as that thought sparked so much dread.

He grabbed what he could. Lentils, a few bags of rice, tinned vegetables and potatoes, and even stuff like tinned chicken in sauce, which wasn't going down too well. Beef jerky, too, and lots of it.

Of course, in time, if he really needed to, he could turn to hunting. That was something he was going to have to consider.

But in a way, that still felt like a surreal admission. It still felt like that wasn't going to happen. That things weren't going to get to that stage.

But then, this whole scenario was bloody surreal, wasn't it?

The sooner he accepted he was stuck in a real shitty situation and prepared for the worst, the better.

Better to be over-prepared than under-prepared.

Of course, things other than food came in handy, too. He was pretty covered where shelter was concerned—he had a good tent back at home and a ton of comfy sleeping bags, so if he had to go out of his way, he was well covered.

He grabbed some first aid supplies. Not just the expected stuff like plasters, painkillers, and suncream—but also stuff like dental floss, too. Dental health was going to be even more important in a world where water supplies were going to be affected and where personal hygiene was going to take a nosedive. But it would also be a useful way of stitching up wounds and tying up as a part of a trap if need be.

It was important to be flexible.

He grabbed a couple more items, like duct tape, a decent-looking water bottle, and a few more essentials that would come in handy, when he turned around.

He looked down to the left. He could hear arguing going down. Some argument over one of the last packets of bacon. He shook his head. Humanity's deadliest moment, and of course, a bunch of overweight pricks were arguing over bacon. That's what humanity was really reduced to in times like these.

"Don't mind them, Harv. You just focus on us, hmm?"

He grabbed more supplies and realised his trolley was full. He needed a rucksack. A proper bug-out-bag. Something to put everything in and carry out of here—something dark coloured, or camo coloured. Something that wouldn't stand out or draw too much attention. He dragged his trolley down the side of the store, and he went to grab one. Started stuffing his supplies into it when suddenly he saw a man standing at the top of the aisle.

It was the shopkeeper or the manager, or whatever they called themselves in this day and age.

There were a few chavvy-looking muscular types near him, grabbing loads of cans of beer, smirks on their faces.

"We—we have a limit," the manager said. "I'm sorry, but that's just how it is, okay? That's just how it is."

One of the men laughed. "And are you gonna stop us, eh?"

The manager, a skinny bloke in glasses, stood there and stared right at them, clearly a little intimidated. "I—I don't want to have to call the police. But if I have to, I will."

The three men all laughed. "Police? Good luck with that one, mate. Come on, Baz. Grab us a bottle of rum while we're at it."

Sam watched this looting go down, watched the manager standing there and staring at them all helplessly. He wanted to go over there. Wanted to tell them to learn some damned manners. Because sure, if this *was* an EMP event—which it sure seemed like—the value of money was very rapidly gonna lose all meaning. Think inflation, only banknotes suddenly being worth absolutely nothing—and only getting worse as supplies grew more and more scarce.

But he could only do what he could. So he'd leave whatever cash he could for the supplies he'd picked up, and he'd hope that was enough.

He went to turn the corner to grab whatever else he could before going down the road and getting a battery for his car when suddenly he heard someone shouting out behind him.

It was the manager. He was lying on the floor. Two of the men had him pinned down and were stripping him of his clothes. One of them was pouring beer over him. They were all laughing like mad.

"Not so tough now, are you?" the man with the beer said. "Fucking piece of shit."

He spat down on the manager and high-fived one of his friends.

Sam stood there and looked at this man on the floor. Looked at how degraded he was. He was crying and shaking, clearly terrified.

He saw these other blokes laughing around him like this was all a joke, and he felt sick.

He couldn't just stand by.

He couldn't just watch this happen.

He clenched his jaw and went to take a step when suddenly, he froze.

The manager lying on the floor, crying.

The laughing blokes around him.

And Harvey beside him.

The supplies on his back.

And the memories.

The heat.

The gunshot

The blood.

Those eyes...

And then Rebecca.

I'm leaving you, Sam. I'm sorry. I've... I've got no choice.

Sam stood there and stared at the dehumanisation of this manager continuing to unfold.

He saw the way these blokes tied his T-shirt around his wrists.

How one of them stood over him now and pissed all over him, laughing all the time.

He saw it all unfolding and knew he couldn't stay here.

He knew this wasn't his fight.

He knew he needed to get away.

He wanted to help the man. He wanted to fight off these thugs and put them in their place.

But he had Harvey by his side.

And he needed to get home.

He felt shame.

He lowered his head.

"Come on, Harvey," he said. "We've got to get out of here."

And then he turned around, left some cash by the abandoned checkout, and walked out of the supermarket and into the pouring rain.

He could still hear the manager begging for mercy when he stepped through the doors.

CHAPTER NINETEEN

Tara couldn't get the dying woman out of her mind.

She was getting closer to the city centre, and things were getting no better. The rain was still hammering down from above. The clouds were thick grey and didn't seem to be thinning. Every now and then, a flash of lightning filled the sky, and for a moment, Tara wondered if the power might be back online. If miraculously, the lights were all going to come roaring back on again, phones would start up again, and news streams would be there to tell everybody what to do and how to react, and the emergency services would be able to run again.

But after every flash of lightning, nothing changed.

After every flash of lightning, there came just another reminder of how bad things were.

Up ahead, she could see smoke rising into the sky. Thick black smoke. She could smell it, too. She didn't know where it was coming from, but she knew a fire in these circumstances was devastating. The rain might just hold it off—just. But not for long. And not forever. Fire was strong and mobile like that.

And without any fire services to save the day... things would get very ugly, very fast.

She could see the train station in the distance. She felt a knot in her stomach. She didn't know why she was still walking. She knew what she'd find when she got the train station. The trains would be stationary. There'd already be a bunch of people there, desperately trying to get out of the city. It'd be panic stations, and it'd be crowded, and it'd be absolute hell.

But still, she kept on walking.

Still, she clung on to that minuscule sense of hope that maybe she'd find some kind of order there. Someone to tell her what she had to do. Police, military, or government—or just *anybody*.

But then, if the phones were out...

Who was giving their orders?

She shook her head.

Just keep walking.

She thought back to that woman who'd died in her car clutching her chest and wondered if that somehow related to the blackout. She said she'd had a heart attack in the past. And she was definitely having some sort of cardiac event. What if whatever had taken the phones offline had taken pacemakers out, too?

She knew how ridiculous she sounded. How far-fetched. Trying to pretend she understood what was going on when really she didn't have the foggiest.

She thought back to the flat.

Thought back to Jonno.

Felt sickness creeping up into her chest.

Panic.

Fear.

A memory she kept on trying to suppress.

A reality she kept on trying to hide from.

If there were no police around, then how long would she be able to get away with what she'd done?

And what if...

No.

She didn't want to think that.

Didn't want to entertain it.

It wasn't possible. She'd seen him lying stationary on the floor. The bleeding was bad. Even if the attack hadn't killed him, it almost certainly would, especially without any ambulances or any kind of help.

The thought of Jonno still being alive scared her more than the thought of him being dead.

That really said a lot about the state of their relationship, didn't it?

But the thought of him being her enemy while he knew what he knew about her...

It didn't bear thinking about.

She walked down the high street, and she kept her head down. The supermarket on her left looked in disarray. The windows were smashed, and the automatic doors were rammed open. People were running out with their arms and trolleys stuffed with all sorts of shit. She could hear a man in there crying out, begging someone for help, and laughter, too. She saw a man with a German shepherd dog step out, met eyes with him for a second.

He looked at her like he knew her, and she did the same thing.

And then she turned and kept on going.

The atmosphere in the city centre was a combination of fear, excitement, and confusion. Some kids cycled around with smiles on their faces like they were enjoying the novelty of this whole situation. People were crammed into bus shelters, whether in hope of a bus turning up out of the blue or simply because they didn't know where else to go right now, she wasn't sure. A homeless man sat under a doorway with a sodden cardboard sign in front of him, and a dog curled up just out of the rain.

It was hard for Tara to put her finger on the general atmosphere. There was something unreal about it. Seeing the city completely powerless and flooded like this was bizarre.

And there was a nervous energy about the place.

A sense that things could deteriorate even further before they got better.

She clambered her way down the street even further, and a part of her wondered why she was even bothering. Even if she did get on that train... she knew how her parents would react to seeing her. How Dad would shake his head, tut. That self-righteous look on Mum's face. *I told you so.*

But then what else did she have?

Where else did she go?

The disappointment. The family failure. The child who'd never lived up to her ballerina sister Emily's billing.

She couldn't remember the last time she'd seen her younger sister. She was in Russia these days as part of a ballet troupe. Or maybe it was Austria now. She couldn't remember. The pair of them had never particularly got along. Mum and Dad had always treated Emily like their favourite and spoke about how proud of her they were—proud of her self-reliance, determination, independence.

And she felt frustrated. Because whenever *she* strove for independence, they seemed to expect things to go south. They always acted with a sense of smug inevitability when they found out she'd got a new job or a new relationship. Always a feeling that she could be doing better for herself.

She pictured the conversation she was about to have.

I've just left an emotionally abusive relationship.

I've no job. I've no home. I've no money. And I've no friends.

Oh. And that Prince Charming boyfriend I was telling you about?

Yeah. About him. I killed him.

She took a deep breath and shook her head.

Yeah, that conversation was going to be a blast.

Especially after...

No.

She didn't need to think about that.

Keep the past where the past belonged.

She walked up the hill towards the train station entrance. Looked down the slope that led towards the station itself. All the black cabs lining either side of the road, shouting at each other, swearing, trying to use their phones even though their phones were quite clearly useless.

"Here goes," she said.

She walked down the slope towards the train station.

Hoping for a miracle.

She stepped inside the doors, out of the rain, relieved for a moment to be sheltered.

And then, when she looked ahead and saw what was unfolding right before her, she realised things weren't just bad.

They were worse than she'd expected.

And this was only the beginning.

CHAPTER TWENTY

Jonno looked down the waterlogged street, and he smiled.

The rain fell heavily from above. Heavier than he'd ever seen it. The water was up to his ankles, which was novel. It reminded him of trips away with the cub scouts. Paddling through streams and rivers. And that time, he'd tied Bobby Westmoreland up to a tree in the middle of the night, stealing his clothes, leaving him to scream alone in the darkness. Everyone feared him back then. Nobody crossed him back then.

Because one wrong look and you could end up another Bobby Westmoreland.

The street was filled with cars. They were all stationary, totally still. Just like that idiot's from earlier. Broken down in the middle of the road. It seemed weird how many of these cars had broken down. His own car wasn't starting, either. And again, it was odd. It was unusual. There was no reason for his car to be broken down. There was no reason for his phone not to be working. There was no reason for *any* of this.

But he could think about that later.

Because right now, there was only one thing on his mind.

Only one person on his mind.

He stood there in the pouring rain, and he couldn't believe how quiet everything was. How silent everything was. Other than the rain. Other than the shouting and arguing. Everything was just so... natural.

And in a way, it was kind of beautiful.

A city without power. A city without electricity.

A city of darkness.

He felt a sharp pain on the back of his head, tasted blood on his lips, and went dizzy again.

He tightened his fists. Closed his eyes. Breathed in deeply.

Keep it together, Jonno. You've made it this far.

He opened his eyes again.

Whenever he opened his eyes, he flashed back to that moment.

The moment in the flat.

The moment he had Tara on the floor.

The moment she swung that bottle around at him and cracked him across the skull.

The moment he woke up and realised exactly what she'd done to him.

Exactly what'd happened to him.

And every time he remembered, he felt that anger again.

That anger towards Tara.

That anger towards that bitch.

After everything he'd done for her.

Everything he'd sacrificed and given up for her.

And how did she repay him?

By refusing his proposal request in a time of grave need for their relationship.

By trying to run away from him.

And then by cracking him over the head with a wine bottle.

Leaving him for dead.

He stood there, looking right down the street, as a crack of light peeked through the clouds.

"Are you okay, sir?'

A man. Short. Bald. Spectacles on his eyes. Standing there and staring at him. He looked a little concerned.

"Your head," the man said. "You're... you're bleeding. Quite badly. The medical centre up the road is taking walk-ins. But—but there's a lot of people. Long queue. Lot of people injured. Who knows what's happening, and who knows when the power's gonna be back? I guess we'd better pray. Better hope for a miracle."

Jonno smiled.

He wiped the blood from his head.

Felt it, warm against his fingers.

And then he looked at the train station in the distance, and his smile widened even further.

There was only one place she'd go.

Only one place she'd run to.

And he knew exactly where it was.

"I think I've found my miracle," he said.

The man frowned. "What?"

Jonno didn't answer.

He just smiled at the man, and he walked towards the train station.

She was going to pay for what she'd done.

CHAPTER TWENTY-ONE

Sam could sense violence on the horizon. It was probably a remnant of his time in the army. A relic from his past. It was hard to explain, difficult to describe. But it was kind of like he had this radar inside him that tuned him into people and situations, and right now, he felt like things were on the verge of spiralling out of control.

He stood outside the little hardware store near the railway station. He could hear loads of shouting inside the railway station. Screaming. It sounded bad, that was for sure. Like things were already getting violent in there.

Not that he was surprised, of course. He knew just how quickly situations could turn violent.

The most ordinary, routine situations could turn right on their head at any moment.

He tensed his jaw.

Closed his eyes.

Took a deep breath as the panic gripped him.

And then he let that fear go, and he opened his eyes again.

The hardware store was called Sparks. Just a little place, independent, but an absolute goldmine. Jeff, who ran the place, was one of the few people Sam actually enjoyed engaging in conversation with these days. He was ex-military too, and they both had an interest in conspiracy theories, in prepper methods, and survivalism. Not a deep obsession about it. Not like these guys in their bunkers over in America. That was a whole different level of commitment.

But between them, they probably knew more than the bulk of the nation.

The hardware store was quiet outside. The bulk of people was swarmed around the train station and the supermarkets. The rain had actually eased a little bit, which was a relief. But judging by that dark grey sky, it definitely wasn't the last of it.

The streets were streaming with running water. People were struggling to stay on their feet. He saw a woman in a white dress digging her heels in, tears rolling down her cheeks as she clutched her screaming baby. He saw car after car after car, and the wreckage of a collision in the distance, smoke rising from it. He could smell more smoke in the air, too. Taste it on his lips. That, and blood. So much had happened in such a short time that it was easy to forget he'd just narrowly escaped a plane crashing towards him with his life intact.

"What a day," Sam muttered.

Harvey whined, presumably in agreement.

Sam felt nerves in his stomach. The situation at the supermarket kept on playing on his mind. Lawlessness had set in extremely quickly—even quicker than he expected. People were fast learning that no sirens were coming, so they were taking any opportunity they had. He remembered the London riots of 2012. How quickly things turned ugly—looting, arson, violence. And how it all proved that law and order was just a myth that everyone subscribed to, that everyone had to believe in for it to work. Or at least the vast majority of people, anyway. It didn't matter if one or two people misbehaved in the grand scheme of things: as long as the majority adhered, it was all good.

But right now, the scales were quite clearly tipped in the favour of lawlessness.

And once people stopped believing in that myth, it would be a very difficult one to instil again.

Especially without the power to do it.

But Sam's plan was simple.

Go into the hardware store.

Grab a battery for his car.

Get back to his car, get it working again, and then get him and Harvey the hell home.

And when he got home, with his rucksack of supplies and all the gadgets and gear he had back there, he'd be set until the storm passed.

He had a few Faraday cages back at home. Faraday cages were basically special containers that prevented electrical signals from passing through, so preserved and protected whatever you put inside from those signals. You could put phones in there, walkie-talkies—anything, really. Obviously, phones relied on masts themselves, most of which would be fried by a solar event, so they were useless, but the principles stood. Faraday cages were fairly easy to build—you could use an old microwave oven and fill it with aluminium if you wanted. Aluminium itself is handy, if it has no holes in it and an insulating layer between its surface and the item being protected.

As for the blackout...

Nerves clawed even harder at his stomach.

Because a large-scale EMP or CME event?

He didn't know how far this went or how widespread it was. But he knew planes were falling out of the skies. He knew cars were crashing. He knew every mobile device and every light in this city was out. And he'd even seen some evidence backup generators were affected back in the supermarket.

His gut instinct?

This was bad.

Really damned bad.

The sooner he got his battery and got home, the better.

He looked down at Harvey, and he nodded.

"Let's go see Jeff and see if he's got anything for us," he said.

He walked up to the door and pushed it open.

As expected, Sparks was quieter than the supermarket.

But even Sam didn't expect it to be quite *this* quiet.

It was silent. Empty. The bell on the door echoed through the store. Sam couldn't hear a thing in here. Not even the creaking of any footsteps. He wanted to call out to Jeff and see if he was here.

But at the same time...

He just wanted to get a battery.

He just wanted to get out of here.

As decent a bloke as Jeff was, Sam was hardly in a mood for small talk right now.

He walked towards the back of the store. He could hear shouting outside. Hear the pouring rain picking up again. It was dark and gloomy in here. The thick dust caught on his chest, making him cough. Harvey looked from left to right, panting, like even he was unsettled by how quiet this place was.

Make no mistake about it; Sparks was never busy. Sam often wondered how Jeff kept this place going. There was no way he could make a living running this place. Jeff shrugged. Told Sam it was a passion project. And every single time he came in here, he had some new, lavish story about how he'd won the lottery, or how he'd discovered he was of royal lineage and received inheritance from aristocracy, or Sam's favourite, he'd replied to what appeared to be a Nigerian scam email and it turned out being legit. One million dollars, all his.

But right now, it was eerie just how quiet it was.

He walked further towards the back of the store when suddenly he heard shuffling behind him.

He stopped.

Looked around.

There was nobody there.

Nothing there.

Sam's stomach tightened with nerves. He'd heard someone. He was absolutely sure he'd heard someone. Definitely sounded like shuffling in here.

But then there was nobody here.

And he couldn't hear anything else.

He shook his head and sighed.

Turned back around.

"Let's get that battery and go, Harv," he said.

He walked closer to the back of the store, and he heard something again.

Something hollow hitting the floor.

Echoing.

Sam froze. Okay, there was someone here. There was *definitely* someone fucking here.

He stood there. Heart racing. Throat growing dryer and dryer by the second.

It reminded him of the army.

Of intercepting the enemy by stealth under cover of darkness.

Of…

No.

Not now.

Don't think about that now.

He squinted over towards where he'd heard that sound. There were two options. Either it was Jeff, and he was laying low. Or it was someone else.

Only one way to find out.

"Jeff?"

No response.

Silence.

Which made Sam even more nervous.

Because if it was Jeff, he'd respond to him. He'd almost definitely respond to him.

He cleared his throat. "Jeff. It's me. Sam. You okay in here, buddy? I just... I just need a battery for my car."

Again, silence.

Not a sound.

So silent that Sam wondered if anyone was in here at all—or if he was just imagining things.

"Okay, bud. I... I really need this battery. So I'm gonna grab it. But I'll leave you some shit under the counter. Probably stuff you've already got anyway, but... but, well. Useful shit. You know as well as I do that money's useless in a world without power. I'll leave you some anyway, though. Just in case it comes back online."

Again, silence in response. So much silence that Sam was beginning to wonder again if there was even anyone here at all.

He turned around.

And then he walked towards that final aisle.

"Not creepy," he muttered. "Not creepy at all."

He walked over to the back aisle, where all the batteries were stored. Made his way down to the middle of it, right to the bottom shelf, where he expected to see his battery.

And then, when he crouched down to grab one, his stomach sank.

There were none in stock.

Out of stock.

"Shit," Sam said. "Typical. Just fucking typical."

He sighed and walked over to the other side of the store. Grabbed a few other bits and bobs. A small fire extinguisher, the use glaringly obvious but rarely mentioned by preppers. A great blunt object to use as a weapon, too, as was the spray—if shit really was hitting the fan as hard as it seemed.

He grabbed a fishing rod, too, which would come in handier than many people gave credit. A decent tent, which he could use if he got caught out tonight. Some zip ties, great for securing gear, helping make shelter, that sort of thing.

And there was something else he grabbed, too. Something he'd forgotten to get from the chemists back at the supermarket. Something unexpected but surprisingly useful.

Condoms.

And no. Not for their usual use. He had no intentions of meeting anyone any time soon.

But they could be filled with water and formed into a lens to start a fire. Or obviously act as a water bottle and hold a couple of litres—as disgusting as it sounded.

And you know what?

The flavouring might make water a bit interesting.

Boring times were gonna call for desperate measures, okay?

He grabbed a few other little tools like compasses and multi-tools, which would obviously always come in handy. Cigarettes, too, not to smoke, but as a useful way of stopping cuts bleeding, easing toothache, stings, fire fuel, that sort of thing. It wasn't ideal. He was facing a very real prospect of a walk back home. And that meant his beloved Land Rover would end up stranded in the middle of nowhere for the foreseeable.

But seeing as he was here, he figured he might as well grab what he could.

He stuffed his rucksack full of essentials and walked over to the counter.

Stopped right in front of it.

Empty.

Quiet.

So unusual.

So... unlike this place.

Unlike Jeff.

Sam reached into his rucksack. He pulled out a few tins and dropped them behind the counter. Then he pulled out a wad of cash and stuffed it onto Jeff's desk. "I've left your payment here, Jeff. Wherever you are... I appreciate it. You stay safe."

Sam went to walk away from the counter when suddenly he heard something.

A click.

The creaking of floorboards.

And shaky breathing.

He froze on the spot.

His heart raced faster.

Someone was behind him.

There was absolutely no denying it anymore.

He turned around.

Jeff was standing there.

His eyes were wide and bloodshot. His long salt and pepper hair was even greasier than ever. He looked... different. Like he was looking at Sam like he didn't recognise him.

And, oh. He was holding a rifle.

"Jeff?" Sam said. "What—"

"Put down that rucksack," Jeff said. "And get out of my store. Right this second."

CHAPTER TWENTY-TWO

Tara thought she was prepared for anything today.

She thought she'd seen everything. Thought there was nothing else that could possibly faze her. She'd killed her boyfriend. She'd held the hand of a dying woman. She'd seen her entire world transform in an instant—transform so much in such a short space of time that things would never go back to normal again, even if the power came back on and the rain stopped falling.

But standing in the train station right now, and staring down at the scene before her, she realised there were still things that could shock her.

A mass of people was in front of her, all gathered around a train on the platform. They were pushing against a wall of police officers, who were trying to get the situation under control. She didn't know if they were trying to get on the train—which clearly wasn't working. She didn't know what they wanted or what they were trying to achieve.

She just knew they were desperate, and they were scared, and tensions were flaring.

And that was dangerous.

Very dangerous.

Further ahead, she saw another train. Only this one was on fire. It'd collided with the back of another train. Must've happened as it was rolling into the station. The windows were smashed. The carriages were all twisted and contorted.

And beside that train, she saw bodies.

Charred bodies.

Lumps of burned flesh.

And suddenly, the entire puzzle of this scene became clear, right before her eyes.

The screaming.

The people on the platform desperately trying to get on board the train.

And the burned bodies lying there on the ground.

They were the families of the people arriving on that crashed train.

They were trying to get on board.

Trying to get to their families.

Trying to find them amidst the chaos.

And the police were stopping them getting on board.

She stood there and looked down towards that train, and she felt sadness inside. Because there was so much devastation. There was so much loss. More than she could wrap her head around. More than she could comprehend.

And it didn't look like the realisation of how much devastation and loss there was would ease any time soon.

She stood there, and she knew there was no point being here in the train station. There was nothing left for her here. She didn't have a way back to her parents', as predicted. There were no buses running. There were no working cars. And there were definitely no trains.

There was no use in her being here.

There was nothing for her here.

And this situation looked like it was getting worse by the second.

She didn't want to be around here when shit really went down.

When violence tipped over the edge.

When things spun out of control.

She didn't know where she was going to go or what she was going to do.

But she knew she couldn't be here.

She knew she needed to get away.

She turned around, and she went to walk out of the train station when suddenly she saw something that froze her to the spot.

Right at the top of the hill leading down to the train station.

Standing there.

Staring at her.

Staring right into her eyes.

Blood trickled down his face.

He looked pale and dishevelled like he wasn't well at all.

And just looking at him sent a wave of nausea crashing over Tara.

Just looking at him made her want to vomit.

Just looking at him made her want to disappear into a hole in the ground.

Because standing there, right at the top of the hill, was someone she recognised.

Someone she recognised very well.

It couldn't be possible.

It couldn't be real.

This had to be in her head.

But the longer she stood there, paralysed by fear, the more Tara realised she wasn't seeing things at all.

This wasn't in her head at all.

Standing there at the top of the hill, Tara saw him.
Jonno.
He was alive.
And he was here for her.

CHAPTER TWENTY-THREE

If there's one thing Sam really didn't expect today—of all the many things he didn't expect—it was to be standing in Jeff's hardware store with a shotgun pointed at him.

Jeff stood right in front of him, shotgun in hand. He was sweating heavily, and his eyes were wide and bloodshot. He was never usually the picture of health. Too many late nights, beers, and video games.

But right now, he looked really bad. The worst Sam had ever seen him.

"Jeff?" Sam said. For a moment, he thought this might be some kind of joke. It had to be, right? He and Jeff had always got along well. They had the same sense of humour and shared the same interests. Sam didn't have many friends these days. "Not many" meaning "none." But sad as it sounded... he'd count Jeff as pretty high on that list of "acquaintances" he actually quite liked.

So seeing him standing here with a shotgun and seeing the look in his eyes... he knew this wasn't a joke. As much as he wanted to believe it was, there was no joke here.

"Throw my shit back on the counter and get out. I won't ask you again."

Sam shook his head. "It's... It's Sam. Jeff, it's me. You know who I am."

"I know who you bloody are, Sam," Jeff said.

"Oh. It's just with... with the frigging shotgun you've got pointed at me. Forgive me for wondering if you'd lost your mind for a moment there."

But Jeff's face didn't change. His expression remained the same. Scared. Like he didn't *want* to be doing what he was doing. But like he knew damn well he had to. "You know how it is, Sam. You and me know better than anyone else around here how it is."

Sam shook his head. "A few supplies. That's all I've got."

"And you know damn well those supplies will run out fast. That when they're gone... they're gone. You've—You've seen how it is out there. You know as well as I do that ain't no ordinary storm. And it ain't no ordinary blackout, either."

Sam's stomach sank. Hearing someone else say the words made it more *real* in a way. It made him feel less crazy. Less like this could be his imagination wild. But it definitely made him more afraid.

Because there was no denying the reality right in front of them.

This was some sort of solar event.

And it was big.

If planes were falling out the sky, if phones weren't working, if cars were grinding to a halt... it was really, really big.

And there was no knowing when the power would come back on.

If the power would come back on.

One thing he'd learned about this country from the pandemic a few years back was that it was grossly underprepared for any kind of major event.

He looked at Jeff, and Jeff looked back at him, and as much as he hated to acknowledge it... he knew Jeff was right.

"I respect you," Jeff said. "And I appreciate you coming here.

I've always appreciated you coming here. I've appreciated your business, and I've appreciated your conversation. But this is serious. The blackout... I saw a helicopter fall from the sky, Sam. It's worse than anything we could've imagined. Like, this is worse than the worst-case scenario."

"We can't know that yet," Sam said.

Jeff frowned. "Don't patronise me, Sam. Don't pretend you haven't seen the things I've seen. Walk away. Walk away right now. Don't... don't let things end nastily between us. I really wouldn't like that."

Sam heard those words, and his stomach sank. He knew there was nothing he could say to Jeff. Nothing he could say to this man he'd considered more than just a shopkeeper to him. This man he'd considered... something like a friend.

"If it was anyone but you, I'd tell you to leave the whole rucksack. But seeing as it's you... just put my stuff back on the counter and go. Now. Before I change my mind."

Sam looked into Jeff's eyes, and he felt sadness deep in his stomach. This whole exchange was a reminder of why he didn't get close to people. On why he didn't trust people.

And a reminder that people often showed their true colours when the shit really hit the fan.

He took a deep breath, and he nodded and smiled.

"Okay," he said. "I'm out of here. Just... just put the shotgun down, though, for Christ's sake. It doesn't suit you."

Jeff glanced at the shotgun like it was some alien object. Then he looked back at Sam, and he smiled nervously. "Yeah," he said. "I guess it was a bit dramatic, wasn't it? But you just never know—"

Sam didn't even hesitate.

He punched Jeff square in the face.

His nose cracked upon contact, and blood spurted out.

And while Jeff was stunned, Sam grabbed the shotgun, cracked him across the face with it again, and he turned it around, and pointed it down at him.

Jeff crouched on the floor, clutching his bleeding nose. Blood oozed out of it like it was leaking from a tap. He looked up at Sam, shock in his wide eyes. "What the—what the hell?"

"I really didn't want to do that," Sam said. "But it's like you said. We're not friends. And it's dog-eat-dog, now. Goodbye, Jeff."

He turned around, grabbed the rucksack over his shoulders, and he walked towards the door of Sparks, Harvey by his side.

"You bastard!" Jeff shouted. "You slippery bastard!"

But as Sam left the store, he didn't feel any accomplishment about what he'd done. He didn't feel any pride about what he'd done.

He felt guilty.

And he felt betrayed.

Just like he'd felt in Iraq.

Just like…

He buried that thought once more as he stepped out of Sparks and into the downpour of rain.

"Come on, Harvey," he said. "Let's go home."

CHAPTER TWENTY-FOUR

Tara saw Jonno standing right there at the top of the road, staring down into the train station and right at her, and she had a horrible sense that she wasn't going to get away from him this time.

He was far away. But it didn't matter. He seemed close. Really close. She'd been so under his influence and in his grasp for years that just looking right at her was enough for her to know that she wasn't in control. That he was coming for her.

And that he was going to get her.

She stood there, frozen to the spot like a rabbit in the headlights. She could hear shouting behind her. The scene at the train kicking off even more as people argued and fought with the police to find their loved ones in that burning wreckage. The smell of smoke was strong in the air. And the taste of sweat was intense on Tara's lips.

But it was Jonno she saw.

It was only Jonno she saw.

Standing there in the rain.

Soaking wet.

Looking right at her with a knowing smile on his face.

She felt sick. Nauseous. Her knees went weak. She could see the blood on his head, and she knew he knew what she'd done. She knew he knew exactly what she'd done to him.

What she was responsible for.

She stood there and looked at him as he looked at her, and she felt torn. Because where did she go? What did she do? Where did she run to?

Her heart raced, and her chest tightened, and she knew she had to get away.

Fast.

There was no time to stick around here. Not anymore.

And then he started walking towards her, and she knew exactly what she had to do now.

She knew she only had one choice.

She turned around and started walking down towards the platforms.

She saw loads of people there, wrestling to get on board, fighting with the police, and she felt crazy. Crazy for walking this way. Crazy for walking into the violence.

But anything was better than standing still.

And anything was better than Jonno finding her.

She looked over her shoulder.

Saw him pacing down the road.

Towards the station.

Fast.

Far faster than she was going.

Shit.

She turned back around and ran down that slope towards the platforms. She could see the train station shop ahead, pulling down its shutters, while a few desperate people ran out with tons of crisps and chocolate bars stuffed in their sodden shirts.

She looked back around again and saw something that made her feel simultaneously relieved and terrified.

Jonno.

There was no sign of him.

He was gone.

She couldn't see him anywhere.

Could she be wrong? Could she be imagining things? Or what if it wasn't him all along?

She didn't know.

She couldn't be sure.

She just knew she didn't have time to waste.

She still had to get away, just to be sure.

She turned around when suddenly she bumped into someone right in front of her.

A police officer. Standing right before her.

Looking right into her eyes.

And her first thought was that it was over. That they'd got her. That they'd got her, and they were going to arrest her, and that she was going to prison, and she was...

And then she remembered Jonno was still alive.

He was still alive, and he was coming for her.

Which meant...

"Can't go any further," the police officer said.

Tara's stomach sank. *Shit*. She cleared her throat. "I... I need to—"

"What you need to do is listen," the man said, a little louder, a little firmer. Sounded like he'd had a really stressful day. "You need to turn around and walk away from here right now. 'Cause nobody else is coming down by the trains. Understand? It's not safe. And there's... there's things down there. Things you don't wanna see. So for your own sake... turn back. Right now. Don't make me cuff you."

Tara felt defeated. She felt broken. And she felt desperate. Because this police officer was in her way—and by standing here, she was in danger. Real danger.

"My... my boyfriend," Tara said. "He's..."

And then she stopped herself.

She stopped herself because she realised how ridiculous she sounded.

How *weak* she sounded.

And that wasn't her.

She was never a weak woman.

It was Jonno who'd made her feel weak.

Who'd made her feel like she wasn't strong.

But that wasn't her.

She wasn't the sort of woman to give up.

She wasn't the sort of woman to be all meek and accept her fate and nod.

Her very rebelliousness was what'd made her such a nightmare to her parents all her life.

She looked into this police officer's eyes and then beyond at the crowd around the train, and she took a deep breath.

"I'm sorry about this," she said.

"What—"

And then she ducked.

Went to run past him.

And that's when she felt the hand on her back.

Dragging her back with immense force.

Pulling her away.

Fuck. He'd stopped her. She'd been too slow. Too slow to sneak past him. He'd grabbed her, and now he was going to arrest her and…

Wait.

The police officer who she'd been arguing with stood right in front of her.

Shaking his head.

Staring at her with wide, pissed-off eyes.

It wasn't him who had hold of her.

So who was it?

And then it dawned on her.

If it wasn't the officer…

She turned around and saw Jonno standing there.

Holding on to her.

Smiling.

"Sorry, officer," he said. "Excuse my wife's manners. She really needs teaching a lesson or two. Don't you, darling?"

CHAPTER TWENTY-FIVE

Sam walked down the street with his bug-out bag over his shoulders and couldn't stop thinking about what'd happened with Jeff.

The rain had eased off a little. The streets were still waterlogged, though. Debris floated along the current. Shopping trollies. Expensive handbags. Mobile phones suddenly useless. It was still so surreal. Still so weird seeing the town so battered by a storm like this. It wasn't something he ever thought he'd witness. Wasn't something he ever thought he'd see.

But then, neither was a massive solar blackout either.

Two items off his bucket list, he figured.

Harvey trotted alongside him, splashing his way through the water. He didn't seem too fussed about it all. Just seemed happy to be out of those vets and safe. Sam was glad he was out of there, too. If he'd been a minute later, God knows what might've happened to him. Sam shuddered at the thought.

"You're here now, boy, huh?" he said. "You're here now. All that matters."

He walked further down the street, out of the thick of the city centre, and he couldn't shake this sense of guilt he was feeling.

Guilt over what'd happened with Jeff back at the store. He wasn't sure why he felt so guilty. Jeff had threatened him, and he'd threatened Harvey, and *anyone* who threatened Harvey was no friend of Sam's.

But he thought back to the moment he'd punched Jeff.

To the moment he'd flipped him onto his arse.

To the moment he'd looked down at him staring up at him as he held his shotgun in hand...

And for that moment, for that one moment, he saw the people he'd let down in Jeff's eyes.

He saw *Iraq* in Jeff's eyes.

Sam's face grew clammy. He didn't want to think about Iraq. He wanted to keep suppressing those memories, just like he'd suppressed them for five years now.

But he wasn't going to be able to suppress them forever.

Those memories were catching up with him.

Fast.

And he wasn't sure he could outrun them much longer.

He saw the stationary cars on the road. Saw a bunch of people queuing outside a medical centre. Some argument going on about God knows what. Probably someone thinking their problem was worse than someone else's. Sounded about right. There were going to be a lot of arguments over the next few days. Weeks. Months. And some of them were going to get deadly.

He knew what would happen if the power didn't come back online—which he was certain it wouldn't, judging by how bad things looked. The few people who were managing to remain sensible and keep their composure were going to wake up tomorrow and realise the power was still out, realise the government or the police *still* hadn't got a hand on the situation, realise they were running low on food and realise everyone was scrambling for supplies, and chaos was going to unfold. It wouldn't take long for looting to become the norm. He'd seen some of it already. And as supplies grew even more scarce, it would only worsen.

And there were the hospitals, too. Overcrowding was already an issue, and after today, it was going to be unmanageable. People would almost certainly be turned away. The car parks out front would become filled with the injured, the sick, the wounded.

And then disease would spread like wildfire.

Sam shuddered. Shook his head. He couldn't concern himself with the problems of everyone else. He needed to focus on the road ahead. The road back home.

It wasn't going to be straightforward. His car was stranded, and the battery was gone, and there was almost no point at all going back to it now.

He felt a twinge of sadness at admitting defeat where his car was concerned.

Thought of those road trips he and Rebecca took. Sometimes, they'd just throw the rucksacks in the back and set off driving somewhere with no real destination in sight at all. Those spontaneous trips made for the best weekends. Set up the tent in the middle of a woods somewhere. Start a fire. Cook marshmallows over it, then fall asleep in the glowing embers, Rebecca lying on his chest, her soft skin against his fingers.

He smiled at the memory. Felt a warmth inside.

And then he felt an emptiness that always accompanied that warmth.

A sadness that always accompanied that warmth.

The memory of what happened next.

Of how quickly things deteriorated and spiralled out of control.

He reached the end of the street. Saw an old man sitting on a park bench, reading a newspaper. The water flowed right past him, over his ankles. He looked unconcerned by what was happening. Like he'd seen it all already, and this was just another day in an unpredictable life.

He hoped that old man got himself away from here sometime soon.

He hoped he got himself home and got himself stocked up with supplies.

He wished he could do more to help everyone...

He turned ahead. Looked at the street in the distance. And at the bridge, which crossed over the river and would take him towards home. It wasn't going to be a short journey, and it wouldn't be an easy one. There were going to be plenty of detours.

But he was going to make it home.

He looked back.

Back at the smoke rising from the high-rise buildings in the distance, the smell of burning strong in the air.

At the stacks of cars sitting in the middle of the street, dead chunks of useless metal now.

He looked at the people heading through the water. Some of them still tapping on their phones in blind, desperate hope.

And then he looked back towards Jeff's store, and he felt a knot in his stomach.

"Whatever happens," Sam said. "I hope you're alright, buddy."

And then he turned back around.

He took a deep breath.

Looked down at Harvey.

Harvey stared up at him and wagged his tail.

"Let's get ourselves back home," he said. "We've got a long way to go."

And then the pair of them started walking.

Up ahead, on the left, he saw a bleeding man dragging a woman out of the entrance to the train station...

CHAPTER TWENTY-SIX

Tara felt Jonno's hand tightening around her arm, and she felt completely terrified.

Blood was trickling down his face. His eyes were bloodshot, and his eyelids were twitching. That big throbbing vein on his temple was larger than she'd ever seen it. It always bulged like that when he was angry.

Looking at it right now, he must be furious.

She felt completely frozen to the spot. Behind her, she could hear the screaming of people trying to force themselves onto that burning train to find their loved ones trapped on there. She could smell smoke in the air. And she could taste sweat and vomit on her lips.

She didn't know what to do. And she didn't want to have to beg anyone for help. She was strong. Far, far stronger than Jonno gave her credit for. And far stronger than she'd fallen into believing herself over the last few years.

But right now, she needed a hand.

She needed help.

She turned around towards the officer she'd tried to get past. "I need..."

Her stomach sank.

The officer was gone.

He'd run over to the train to help with a scuffle.

There were no other police officers near her.

And everyone in this crowd was so caught up in their own shit that none of them were paying her any attention.

"Come on," Jonno said. "It's not safe in here. Let's get out of here. Somewhere a little more... private."

Tara felt fear creeping from head to toe.

He was going to put her through hell for what she'd done to him.

But she had to stand tall.

She had to stay strong.

She tried to drag her arm away. "Let go of me."

Jonno tightened his grip so hard that she could feel one of his rings digging into her bony wrist.

"You're hurting me," Tara said.

Jonno shook his head. Smiled. "I'm hurting you? *I'm* hurting *you*? After what you did to me? Leaving me a note to say you're leaving me after all these years. And then... and then *assaulting* me? Leaving me for dead? And *I'm* the one hurting *you*? No. No, I've had it, Tara. I've had it with your emotionally abusive shit. We need a serious conversation about how things are going to be between us. Right now."

He pulled her so hard she felt her arm almost popping out of its socket.

Her face burned with rage. *Her* the emotionally abusive one? And he thought he had any right to get on his high horse right now? Piece of shit. Absolute piece of shit.

She dug her heels into the ground, tried to stand firm. "There is no *us*," she said. "Not anymore. So let me go. Let me go, or I'll scream at the top of my fucking lungs right now, you abusive monster."

"Scream all you fucking want," he said. "*Everyone's* screaming.

Nobody'll bat an eyelid."

Tara took a deep breath. "I think I'll take my chances."

She went to let out the biggest damned scream of her entire life when she suddenly felt something sharp against her stomach.

She looked down and could barely believe what she was looking at.

Jonno had a knife pressed to her stomach.

Right against her skin.

She looked up at him. Frowned. "What..."

Jonno smiled. "You think you are the only one who can play dirty, hmm? No, no. The rules changed when you battered me with that wine bottle, missy. Now come on. Let's get out of here. We need to talk. Unless you want me to stick this inside you. Although with no hospitals or medical treatment right now... I'm not sure that's a situation I'd want to be in."

Tara's surging confidence slipped again. Fear took over once more. He was willing to stab her. He was willing to stab her right here in the middle of the train station.

And something about that frenzied look in his eyes made her pretty sure he wasn't bluffing, either.

She felt torn.

Torn between standing her ground. Between showing the strength she knew she had—that she knew she'd *always* had.

And between stepping down.

Getting out of here.

At least if she looked like she was following Jonno's wishes, she might find an opportunity to sneak away from him when he was least expecting it.

"Okay," she said.

Jonno's eyes widened, as did his smile. "Good," he said. "That's more like it."

He turned her around then, forcefully, and pushed her up the slope, back towards the train station exit. She saw so many faces walking past her. A bulky man in a high vis jacket covered in blood and tears. A woman holding a screaming baby. Two security guards racing down towards the train wreckage, desperate to get things back under control.

She saw all these people running by and just needed one of them to help her. She just needed to get the attention of one of them, and then maybe she'd be okay. Maybe she'd find her way out of this mess.

Always so reliant on other people...

Always relying on others to clean up your mess...

Mum's voice. Loud in her ears.

She didn't want to believe her.

She didn't want her to be right.

But as Jonno pushed her further and further out of the station, and as the opportunity to get anyone else's attention rapidly faded, she realised her mother was probably right.

And right now, maybe that wasn't such a terrible thing after all.

She caught the eye of a taxi driver up ahead. He looked at her, right at her. If she just mouthed the word "help," then maybe he'd help her right now. Maybe he'd realise she was in danger.

Maybe he'd come to her aid.

She went to open her mouth when suddenly, Jonno swung her to the right and pushed her down the alleyway to the side of the train station.

She tried to scream, but he covered her mouth.

She tried to wriggle free, but he pressed the full force of his body up against her.

He lifted that knife to her neck, and he smiled.

"Now," he said. "It's time we taught you a thing or two about manners."

CHAPTER TWENTY-SEVEN

Tara felt Jonno's blade against her throat, and she started to think this might actually be the end.

Jonno's eyes were bloodshot, angry red. His temple throbbed like the vein was trying to burst out of his skull. Sweat and blood drenched his face. He looked mad. Really frigging mad. There were times when he was mad that she was able to get through to him. To bargain her way towards winning him around and staving off his mood.

But right now, Jonno looked beyond winning over.

Jonno looked completely possessed with anger, fury, and self-righteousness.

He hated being embarrassed. Didn't even like it if she teased him in public. She remembered she'd once squeezed him and kissed him in front of a bunch of people walking down Blackpool promenade, and he'd physically recoiled. Told her he found it embarrassing and childish. Later on, he said he was just having a bit of a rough day and that he loved her, and he made sure to kiss her and make a fuss of her in public the next time they were out.

Looking back, she should have seen the red flags.

So many red flags.

So many signs.

He hated being embarrassed.

And she'd made a fool of him.

Majorly made a fool of him.

Attacked his pride.

And he didn't look the sort of guy who would just let that go right now.

He squeezed her mouth so tight. She tried to breathe, but it was difficult. She felt faint. Nauseous. Sick. Felt like she was going to pass out. She felt panic creeping up into her chest, threatening to take over.

But she couldn't pass out.

Not now.

Not in this situation.

Because God knows what Jonno would do to her if she passed out.

"You insult me by writing that letter," Jonno said. "You insult me by rejecting my proposal. After everything I've done for you. After everything I've given up for you. And then you insult me by walking away from me. And then when I *try* being reasonable and communicating with you... you attack me. Leave me for dead. What kind of a monster are you?"

Tara couldn't believe this prick was actually gaslighting his way into making out *he* was in the right.

He'd emotionally abused her.

And he'd physically abused her today, too. Pinning her down on the lounge floor.

If she hadn't attacked him, God knows what would've happened to her, or where she'd be right now.

She shook her head. Tried to wriggle free of his grip. Tried to gasp for a breath behind that heavy hand as all the while, water powered down the alleyway, as people in the city screamed, and as the smell of smoke grew stronger.

"You can try and worm your way out all you like, princess," Jonno said. "I'm done being lenient with you."

He pushed so hard against her mouth that she felt her teeth digging into the backs of her lips.

And she found herself wanting to beg.

Please, Jonno. Please. Let me go. Let me...

And then she felt that strength inside her once more.

That *fight* inside her once more.

She narrowed her eyes.

She opened her mouth so she could taste the sweat on his palm.

Pressed her teeth against his skin.

And then she bit down on Jonno's palm.

Hard.

His eyes widened.

He let out a yelp.

He dragged his hand back, away from her mouth.

"Bitch," he said. "You're a nasty, violent bitch; that's what you are."

"Get your fucking hands off me," Tara said.

Jonno grabbed her again. Around the throat this time. He was so close to her face she could smell the sweat on his skin and his nasty breath. "I didn't know you had it in you. But I should've seen it coming. You've been acting up for months now. I'm starting to think there's something wrong with you. And that you need really looking after."

Tara spat in Jonno's face. "The only thing wrong is you."

He let go of her neck. Wiped the spit away from his face. Looked at it, there on his hand. And then he wiped it against Tara's shirt and looked at her from head to toe with disgust. His cheeks flushed. He looked even more pissed.

Pissed enough to attack her, right here in public?

Nothing was off the table at this point.

As terrified as she was, she stood tall and stared this monster right in his eyes. "You can tell yourself whatever stories you want to tell yourself at this point. It's over, Jonno. You and me are finished. And nothing changes that. Nothing. If you've got any self-respect... if I meant anything at all to you, and if our relationship meant anything at all to you, you'll walk away. Now."

Jonno stared at her. Quiet. Like he was really thinking through his next move.

He stared even longer. Time dragged on. Felt like it was lasting forever.

And then, finally, he took a deep breath, and he sighed.

"When the power comes back on, I'm going to phone the police. I'm going to get you done for attempted murder."

"And I'll be fucking delighted to be locked in a cell away from you."

He blinked. Stepped back a little. Like those words shocked him.

And then he smiled the most sinister smile she'd ever seen.

He pressed the knife to her throat.

"You know you'd never see the light of day again. Not after what you did in your past."

A knot in Tara's stomach.

That smirk on his face.

He wouldn't, would he?

He pressed the blade against her throat.

"Or, I could take you back home and make a nice little cell for you there."

He pressed the blade further to her neck.

So close it stung.

"And there's no police to call. There's no friends to call. There's no family to call. Because they all hate you. They're all fed up with you. All you have is me. All you're relying on is me. And that's going to get a whole lot more apparent for you, darling. You're going to realise just how lucky you've been. Especially with what I know about you."

Tara looked into the eyes of a man she couldn't believe she'd fallen in love with. As much as she wanted to maintain her composure, as much as she wanted to be strong... she felt afraid.

"Now come on," he said. "Let's get you back home."

He went to grab her by the hair and drag her away when suddenly, Tara heard footsteps, right at the entrance of the alleyway beside her.

She looked around.

Jonno looked around.

A man was standing there.

Tall. Muscular. Dark-haired. Blue eyes. Rucksack over his shoulders.

There was a German Shepherd dog by his side.

"Is everything okay here?" the man asked.

CHAPTER TWENTY-EIGHT

"Is everything okay here?" Sam asked.

He'd seen this bloke dragging the woman out of the train station. He could tell from how tight he was holding her arm that she wasn't comfortable. And then the way he jolted her down that alleyway at the side of the station, out of sight.

As much as he knew he should just stay far away, and as much as he knew he should keep his fucking beak out... Sam couldn't just stand by and watch.

He couldn't just let potentially abusive shit go down when it was happening right in front of him.

He'd seen some horrible things already today—and in his life in general. And there were times he could've helped people today, and he chose not to. Moments he regretted.

He wasn't sure why this woman was different. Why this situation was different.

Maybe it was the shit that went down with Jeff. A bit of guilt over how that ended.

Or how he'd failed to save the receptionist at the vets.

Or the manager in the supermarket, taunted and teased.

Helpless.

He wasn't sure what it was.

But something made him follow that woman and that abusive-looking thug.

Something brought him here.

And he was beginning to realise that this really was a serious situation.

The man had a knife to the woman's neck. He was a bruiser. A real meat-head, by the looks of things. Covered in sweat. And from the looks of things, blood.

And then the woman. She was pale. Dark circles under her eyes. She looked like she'd been through some shit. At the hands of this creep? He wasn't sure. But judging by the look of this guy, probably.

"Wait a second," the man said. "I... I know you."

Huh? This guy knew him? He must be mistaken. Sam made sure he didn't associate with pricks like this. He made sure he didn't associate with *anyone* in general as a rule of thumb.

But this prick?

No chance.

Absolutely no chance at all.

He went to tell him he must be thinking of someone else when suddenly, it clicked.

The meat-head.

The meat-head who'd dragged him out of his car earlier today. Which felt like fucking forever ago.

The man who'd thrown him onto the rainy ground and punched him.

Gym Boy.

"You," Sam said.

Gym Boy smirked. Shook his head. Kept holding on to the woman. "Either you've got a fucking death wish," he said. "Or you're gonna turn around, right now, and mind your own business. What's it gonna be?"

Sam felt anger towards this prick. Where he was just an

annoying bastard with a chip on his shoulder before, seeing him being physically aggressive towards a woman made him hate the cunt. Beside him, Harvey growled.

He looked at the woman. Her eyes were wide. She didn't look... *afraid*. She was clearly no damsel in distress.

She just looked a bit in shock about the whole situation.

"Hey," Gym Boy said. "Eyes away from her and on me. Turn around and walk away. Or did you not get the message earlier?"

"You weren't beating a woman earlier," Sam said. "That changes things."

Gym Boy's face turned sour. He went red. He looked at the woman, then back around at Sam.

And then he took the knife away from the woman's neck and pointed it towards Sam.

"I don't know if I need to spell this out to you, mate. Clearly you're a bit tapped to still be around here. But this is between me and my girlfriend, alright?"

"I'm not your girlfriend."

Gym Boy turned around. Frowned. "What?"

The woman narrowed her eyes and looked at the man with such a strong hatred it actually made Sam wonder if she'd ever loved this guy. "It's over between us, Jonno. Just like I told you it was. So get off me. Get off me right this second. I don't care if the power's out. I don't care what you'll say or what you'll do. You need to get the hell off me right now."

Gym Boy—Jonno—looked stunned. He shook his head. Then looked around at Sam.

"You heard the woman," Sam said. "Get off her. Unless you want there to be trouble."

Jonno narrowed his eyes. He opened his mouth like he was going to say something. Held that knife in the air, shakily hovering it between Sam and the woman.

And then he smiled.

Smiled right at Sam.

"Is this him then, Tara?" he asked. "Is he the one you've been fucking? He the real reason you think you're leaving me?"

"Trust me," Tara said. "I don't need a good reason to leave you. And you'd know if I was fucking anyone else, you stalker creep."

He slapped her. Hard across her face.

Anger intensified inside Sam.

He stepped forward.

Tensing his fists.

He was in Iraq again.

He was feeling the anger again.

The need to do something.

The need to intervene.

The need to act.

The need to—

Please!

And then Jonno threw Tara towards the floor.

Right to Sam's feet.

He looked down at her. Tears started flooding down his cheeks. "You can have her, mate. You can fucking have her. But this is not over. By any stretch of the imagination."

Sam walked past her.

He was going to choke this fucker.

He was going to throttle him.

He was going to kick the shit out of him for what he'd...

And then he felt a hand.

A hand on his leg.

He looked down.

Saw the woman, Tara, climbing off the floor.

Holding him back.

"Leave him," she said. "Please. Don't... don't give him any excuse to hate me even more than he already does."

Sam looked back at Jonno.

Looked right into those eyes.

Right at that smirk of his.

Like he was goading him.

Like he was *trying* to get him to punch him.

He took a deep breath.

Tried to calm himself down, using the methods he'd learned in counselling.

Focused on his breath.

Let everything else pass through his consciousness like clouds in the sky.

"Go on," Jonno said, knife in hand. "Do whatever you have to do, prick. Or are you too much of a coward to even do that?"

Sam tightened his fists.

One punch. One fucking good punch. That's all he needed.

"Please. Just leave him. Please."

Sam took a deep breath.

"Come on," Sam said. "Let's get the fuck out of here."

He walked away with the woman, Tara.

Walked away, keeping his eyes on Jonno at all times.

Standing there with the knife in his hand.

Blood trickling down his face.

"This isn't over," Jonno said. "You might think it's over. But it's only just getting fucking started."

"Good luck with that," Sam said.

And then he walked around the corner with Tara and Harvey, and away from the train station, towards whatever awaited them.

CHAPTER TWENTY-NINE

Tara walked alongside this stranger, and for some inexplicable reason, she felt completely safe in his presence—and completely comfortable.

And she didn't even know his name yet.

They'd been walking for about ten minutes now. Or maybe it was longer than that. Just walked up and out of the train station, then both took a left and made their way out of the city, as simple as that. Tara couldn't stop looking over her shoulder. Couldn't stop thinking about Jonno's last words to her.

"This isn't over. You might think it's over. But it's only just getting fucking started."

And the thought sent a shiver down her spine.

Because she thought she'd killed him. She thought he was dead. And still, he'd found a way to hunt her down. To follow her.

She thought she'd escaped him once already... but he'd found her.

But every time she looked back, she didn't see anyone following. Sometimes she'd see people walking along or running towards her, and for a horrifying moment, fear would kick in. Because she was convinced it was him.

But it was never him.

Never.

She turned around and looked at the man and the dog beside her.

He was tall. Well-built. Probably a few years older than her, but hard to tell. He had a maturity about him. A few greys sprinkled through his dark hair. A little bit of stubble and dark skin, which would no doubt tan well in the sun. He was serious. Didn't look like the sort of bloke who smiled or joked much.

The dog he was with was gorgeous. A lovely German Shepherd. Tara loved dogs. She'd always wanted one as a kid, but her parents convinced her she could barely even look after herself.

Naturally, they'd gifted her sister Emily one for her eighth birthday. A little chihuahua called Sandy. And when Emily got bored of her, it was Tara who ended up feeding her, walking her, and spending all her time with her. Not that she minded. She'd always wanted a dog.

Sandy ran off one day. Emily left the gate open like a fucking little idiot, and she bolted. And Tara was devastated. More devastated than Emily. Because she was the one who cared for that dog. She was the one who looked after her. She was the one who'd made the stronger bond with her. And she was the one who picked up her shit.

She remembered telling Mum and Dad about what'd happened. And the pair of them blamed her for it. Grounded her for three months and only let her leave her room for food and water. No television. No games. No bike rides. No fun at all. Nothing.

And little Emily absolutely loved it.

She thought about the threat Jonno made. The one of locking her up like she was some kind of prisoner. She'd been there before already.

Why did she always end up in situations like that?

She looked up and saw the man looking at her.

She felt a little embarrassment for being caught looking. Her cheeks flushed, which was a fucking awful glitch of nature, wasn't it? Nobody wants the other person to know when they're embarrassed. So naturally, everyone's faces turned bloody crimson when they were embarrassed. God's joke, right there.

She cleared her throat. Looked away a second, back to the road ahead. Then when she'd regained a little composure, she looked back at him. "He's a lovely dog."

The man nodded. Looked away. "Thanks."

Tara cleared her throat some more, something that was becoming a bit of an annoying habit. "I... I wanted to say thanks. For the help back there."

"Don't mention it," the man said.

"I'm... I'm Tara. Do you have a name?"

Do you have a name? What the hell was she even asking?

"I do," he said.

"And..."

The man sighed. Sounded like she was getting on his nerves. "Sam."

"Sam. Nice to meet you. And your dog?"

"Harvey."

"Harvey. Nice... nice to meet you too."

Harvey wagged his tail. Far friendlier than his owner, that was for sure.

She didn't know where to go from here. She knew where she *had* to go. Back to her parents. But that was a journey she would take by foot by the looks of things.

And a journey on foot up to the Lake District?

That wasn't all that compelling right now.

She glanced at Sam and wanted to ask if she could join him. If she could go with him. But at the same time, she felt this hurdle. This strange bridge between them stopping her from asking.

"I'm... I'm guessing you're heading out of the city," Tara said.

"It would appear so, wouldn't it?"

Tara nodded. "I've got to head north. Arnside."

"Arnside," Sam said. "Nice place. Long way."

God, was this guy conversationally retarded or something? "Yeah. It's a shame I can't hail an Uber or something, right?"

Sam nodded. Not a glimmer of humour about him.

Miserable git.

"I... You don't mind if I walk with you for a bit, do you? It's just... well. I'm heading this way anyway. And..."

She didn't want to admit why she wanted to walk with him.

The prospect of Jonno following her.

She didn't want to give this stranger the satisfaction of knowing she felt safer with him. Because she was a strong woman. An independent woman.

And she didn't want to admit something else, either.

Something a little embarrassing.

Something...

Well.

She found Sam alluring. First impressions and all, but there was something about him she found interesting.

Shit. She'd only just left Jonno today. What kind of slut did that make her?

Trust her to fall for someone on day one of the end of the fucking world.

He looked around at her. Stared into her eyes with those crystal blue eyes of his. He looked like he wanted to argue. Like he wasn't sure.

And then he just said: "I don't see why not."

Tara nodded. She smiled.

It might not be first-date fireworks.

But it was something.

She looked back over her shoulder at the city one last time.

She swore she saw movement heading her way.
A silhouette, somewhere in the distance.
But it was probably just her mind playing tricks on her.
Probably.

CHAPTER THIRTY

Jonno watched Tara and that man walk away, and he felt hatred boiling within.

He looked down the road towards them as they walked away, side-by-side. His face burned hot. Not just at Tara for humiliating him. But at this cunt for stepping into his life and taking her away from him, too.

He should've punched him a little harder when he'd dragged him out of his car earlier.

He should've punched him so hard that he never got up again.

The clouds were still thick and grey, but the rain was easing. The roads were still full of water and stationary cars. People wandered past aimlessly, lost. He could hear footsteps splashing through the water. See men, women, and children walking hand in hand, rucksacks over their shoulders. He could see all kinds of signs that the world as he knew it just hours ago had changed—and it'd changed in a big way.

But he couldn't shift his focus from the man.

From his dog.

From Tara.

He watched them walk away, and he felt sick with rage and

anger. The bitch had humiliated him. The pair of them had humiliated him. And besides—Tara didn't get to decide to just walk away. She was *his*.

And he knew how that sounded. He knew if he sat down with a therapist, they'd probably tell him he was insecure, controlling, and manipulative... but he didn't see it that way.

Because those therapists wouldn't have been in a relationship with Tara.

They didn't know what it was like.

What *she* was like.

What she'd *done*.

Tara needed someone like him to keep her on track.

Without him, she was a danger to herself and others.

That was it. That's all it was.

It was nothing to do with manipulation.

It was nothing to do with control.

Watching her walk away with this man, his heart thumped harder in his chest. She'd been cheating. He was absolutely sure of it. He wasn't sure *how* because he checked her phone after she'd used it. And he had a Tile tracker on her keys too, so if she *did* leave the house, he knew where she'd been and how long she'd been there. All kinds of possibilities spiralled his mind. Maybe she'd found the tracker and figured out a way to get around it. Or maybe he'd just miscalculated. He wasn't sure. He really didn't know.

He just knew that she was clearly fucking this prick.

And for that, he had to pay, too.

He looked down at the man and his dog and Tara.

Felt the hatred inside his body.

And he smiled.

He was going to hunt them down.

He was going to make them pay for what they'd done to him.

CHAPTER THIRTY-ONE

Sam walked down the rain-swept road towards his home and had no idea how to small talk with this Tara woman beside him.

The further he got out of the city, the more certain he became that this was definitely some kind of EMP event. Not that he ever doubted it when he was back in the city. All the signs were there: the mass outages, the planes falling from the skies, and the cars sitting stationary in the middle of the streets.

But there was some small, limited fraction of himself that wondered if maybe, just maybe, the blackout might be confined to the radius of Preston city centre somehow. If once he got out of the city centre, he might find that power returned—however unlikely and miraculous an idea that may be.

Turned out he was bullshitting himself.

Because shit was just as bad outside the city.

If not worse.

The skies were getting darker, too. And that was worrying. So many people displaced, far from home, forced to sleep in their cars or attempt to make it back amid all these floods. Looting and lawlessness breaking out across the city. Tensions were going to erupt. Disorder was going to be even more widespread.

And when people woke up tomorrow and realised that the power outage was indeed still a thing and that they were still far from home, not only that but they were even hungrier and even thirstier and even more desperate for food and water and shelter than they were when they went to sleep...

Yeah. Sam wanted to be far away from the more urban side of town when that all kicked off.

He clutched his rucksack tightly to his shoulders as he walked down the road. He saw people looking at him, peering out at him through their car windows. So many wide-eyed, grey-faced expressions. And some of them looking at his rucksack, clearly wondering if there was something in there worth grabbing. It wasn't evil or anything like that. At the end of the day, humans were an inherently selfish breed. That selfishness had got the species to heights it wouldn't have reached if it wasn't so selfish.

At the end of the day, if you have a kid who desperately needs food, and you see a man wandering along with a rucksack full of supplies... you're gonna do whatever you've got to do.

Sam knew it wasn't personal.

But likewise, he was going to fight, too.

He glanced around at the woman, Tara. Saw her looking at him, then turning away. She wasn't saying much. And he was kind of pleased about that. Small talk wasn't his forte. It hadn't been for a long time. He kind of hadn't needed it because he didn't have anyone to small talk to.

And in a way, he preferred it that way.

He missed it sometimes. Missed walking with someone by his side. Missed laughing at funny shit and having someone to share it with.

But the way he saw it... this was his punishment.

This was his penalty.

For what he'd done.

He remembered what Rebecca used to say right before she left him. *You really need some therapy, Sam. This can't go on. Not like this...*

And as much as Sam knew she was right... he just couldn't.

Because therapy would dig up the memories he didn't want to excavate.

And he wasn't sure he could handle those memories.

He looked down at Harvey, who seemed to be enjoying paddling through the water alongside him, and he smiled.

At least he had his loyal pup with him.

His lifesaver.

"So, do you have any family, or..."

Tara's voice took Sam by surprise. He turned around. She wasn't looking right at him. More at his body, staring into space somewhat. Like she was finding this entire exchange uncomfortable, too. "I mean... yes. And... well. Yes and no."

Tara raised an eyebrow and looked right at him now. "You're not one for straight answers, are you?"

"I just don't see what my family has to do with anything."

"It's just... small talk. That's all."

"Well I'm not good at small talk."

"That much is clear."

Sam's cheeks flushed. He turned around from her and kept walking. He was glad he'd saved her from that creep. But the sooner their paths diverted, the better.

"I am grateful," Tara said. "For what you did back there. I mean... I'd love to say I had it. I'm really not the damsel in distress type. But I needed a hand back there. He's a piece of work. And I'm... I think he might've killed me. I really think he might've killed me. So thank you. Really."

Sam nodded. "Like I said. Least I could do."

"A lot of people would've just walked by. And don't say they wouldn't. I've done it myself. Seen a few people arguing in the street. And the last thing you do is get involved. We do the typically British thing and lower our heads and walk on by and pretend everything is right in the world. And then the next day we're seeing the news some woman's been murdered by another man, and we wonder why we're in so much shit."

Sam shrugged. "I guess I couldn't just leave you."

"And I respect that. Truly."

Sam knew he should feel flattered by the woman's gratitude. He appreciated it.

But instead, he felt guilt.

Guilt for the times he hadn't been able to save people.

Guilt for the times he should have tried to help.

Guilt for the times he knew he could have helped others, and he hadn't.

And why?

Why hadn't he just tried?

That question would haunt him for the rest of his life.

"Can I ask you a question?" Tara asked.

"You just did," Sam said.

"This blackout. You seem... you seem to have an idea about what's going on. If you don't mind me saying."

"I mean, I think I have an idea. Based on what I've seen."

"Mind sharing a bit of that knowledge of yours?"

Sam looked at her. And he hated that he was going to have to break the news to her about what was happening here. Most people weren't going to be prepared for how things would deteriorate. Most people weren't ready for what Sam had to say. And maybe that's why this blackout had struck in silence. Maybe it was a solar event. Maybe the government knew about it, and they'd just chosen to suppress the truth because they knew the kind of damage and destruction that truth could cause.

Or maybe they were just as ignorant and clueless as the rest of the country.

The rest of the world.

He told Tara everything. Everything he knew about EMPs and

CMEs. Everything about the Carrington Event of the 1800s. Everything about the devastation a solar storm of that size would cause in today's interconnected world. Everything about the threat from rival powers and about just how much devastation and destruction would unfold: GPS, satellite, and the electrical grid.

And he told her how, if it was as big as he thought it was... the city, and potentially the country and the world, wasn't coming back from this any time soon.

He even told her about some of the supplies he'd gathered. Including the dental floss, which she seemed to find rather amusing, and viewed with some cynicism.

Tara stared back at him, wide-eyed, not saying a word. "So, to summarise. Just for the uneducated. What you're saying, if I've been listening correctly... is that most of the country and quite possibly a large chunk of the planet is completely and utterly fucked? And that those who aren't quite as completely and utterly fucked—people like yourself, who happen to know a few survival tricks—are probably still by the law of odds also completely and utterly fucked?"

Sam smiled. He couldn't help himself. He actually laughed a little, too, which felt odd. It felt unfamiliar. "Yeah," he said. "Good to know you've been listening."

Tara smiled back at him. Shook her head. "Well. This is a bit of an odd first conversation, isn't it?"

He looked into her eyes, and he felt something inside him. He felt a relic of happiness resurfacing. He found her attractive. Beautiful, in fact. He wanted to ask her to come home with him. Ask her to shelter there with him rather than trekking up to Arnside on her own—a journey that, without being patronising towards her, would be tough for anyone in these conditions.

He looked at her and wanted to ask her so much when he suddenly felt that brick wall crash into him.

That emotional block heightening.

That tension.

That fear.

Those memories of love.

And those memories of loss.

His smile dropped, and he looked away.

"Come on," he said. "You... you can, erm. You can grab some supplies. From mine. Before... before the rest of your journey. I'll have a few things for you that you can take. As long as you return them when the power comes back on."

Tara raised her eyebrows and smiled. "After everything you've just told me, I'm not sure I'll ever need to return them."

"If you don't, your psycho boyfriend isn't the only person who'll have it in for you."

"Psycho *ex*-boyfriend," Tara said.

Sam nodded. Shook his head.

"What?"

"It doesn't matter."

"No. Go on. I've got you talking at last. Don't shut up now."

"I just... You seem pretty... great. You know."

"That's very kind of you. The jury's still out on you, but I'm sure we'll get there."

"I just... That guy. I don't understand how..."

"How I ended up trapped with him? Yeah. Sometimes I wonder that myself. But these things don't happen overnight. They happen slowly, you know? What doesn't seem like a red flag at the time is a red fucking planet stuffed with red flags in hindsight. And besides. Love can be blinding, as cheesy as it sounds."

"That did sound a little cheesy."

"You don't strike me as the sort of man who's really subscribed to all those lovey-dovey romantic notions, if you don't mind me saying."

A tension in Sam's chest.

Rebecca's laughter in his ears.

He gulped. And he looked away. His heart racing. His breathing growing more laboured.

"Sam?" Tara said.

"Come on," Sam said, starting walking through that running water again. "We can't stand around here forever."

"Did I say something—"

"Just... just come on, okay? It's... it's just like I said. We head back to mine. I'll get you some supplies. And then..."

He didn't want to finish.

He didn't want to say the words.

But deep down, he knew he couldn't stay with Tara.

Deep down, he knew there was only one way he could be.

Alone.

CHAPTER THIRTY-TWO

Tara really didn't know what to make of Sam.

They'd been walking for a fair while now. Had to be an hour or so. The clouds weren't as thick, and the rain wasn't as heavy, but it seemed darker, so it must be getting later in the day. The thought of nightfall made her shiver. She'd seen some pretty grim sights today so far. And if what Sam said was true—and she had no reason to doubt the conclusions he'd come to—things wouldn't get any better overnight. They were going to get worse.

And when the whole country woke up tomorrow and realised they were *still* without power...

That was a recipe for disaster.

The rain wasn't falling as heavily, but it was still up to her ankles. All around her, she saw the sights that she was growing familiar with. Cars sitting there in the middle of the street, some of them still occupied, some of them abandoned. There weren't as many around here. The kind of suburban, country-ish lane that not many people came down.

She looked over her shoulders. Back down the road they'd walked.

She couldn't stop thinking of Jonno.

The look of anger in his eyes.

And that smile.

That smile on his face.

And the thought of it just made her shudder.

He'd looked at her in some pretty nasty ways before. She wasn't a stranger to him making her feel like dirt or looking at her with disgust.

But there was something different to how he'd looked at her before, when she'd walked away with Sam.

He looked at her like he hated her.

He looked at her like he might actually kill her.

And that scared her.

She turned back around and saw Sam looking at her.

He looked at her differently to Jonno. She saw it right away. There was a softness to his expression. An inquisitiveness. And while he had a hard exterior, she could tell there was a whole world of complexity and depth underneath the surface.

She wanted to know why he'd freaked out when she brought romance into the mix. She'd mentioned something about not thinking he'd be a romantic type, and his face dropped right away. She wanted to ask him about it. But she didn't want to piss him off any more than she already had. He was letting her join him, after all. He was going to let her stock up on supplies when they got to his home.

And then...

Well. It was time for her to stop leaning on people, and it was time for her to make her own way back to her parents.

But she had to admit, there was something about Sam that deeply intrigued her.

She watched him walking, Harvey by his side. Walking with this tall, confident demeanour. None of the panic that seemed to curse anyone else she'd seen since the blackout. Just cool, calm composure.

She went to open her mouth and ask him something—anything—about himself, and about his past, and about why he'd reacted the way he had just earlier when she heard something that sent a shiver up her spine.

A muffled cry.

She stopped.

Looked over at the block of flats to her right.

"Do you hear that?" she asked.

Sam slowed down. Frowned. "I don't hear anything. Come on. Let's keep going."

Tara didn't budge.

She stayed stood there.

Stared at that block of flats.

"I... I swear I heard..."

And then she heard it again.

Another muffled cry.

"Help! Someone—someone help me!"

Tara's stomach sank.

She turned around to Sam.

"Still don't hear that?"

Sam's eyes narrowed.

And then he did something Tara didn't expect.

He lowered his head, and he started walking away.

"It's... it's not our business. Come on. Let's get going. We're getting closer."

Tara felt shocked. What the fuck? She didn't expect that of Sam. Especially not after he'd helped save her.

Because as much as she wasn't some damsel in distress, and as much as she hated the idea of needing saving somehow... she *had* relied on Sam to help her out of that shitty situation with Jonno.

She had no idea where she'd be right now if he hadn't shown up.

So the fact he was choosing to ignore a cry right now made her feel so, so fucking disappointed.

"What the hell?" Tara asked.

Sam kept on walking. "If we stopped to help everybody, we'd be here all day. Come on."

Tara shook her head, puffed out her lips. "You stopped to help *me*."

"That's... that was different."

"Why was that different?"

"Look," Sam said, turning around. And for the first time, Tara saw a slip in his composure. "If you want to go on some fantasy quest at saving everybody, then be my guest. You're your own person. I offered you some supplies. I offered you some help on your journey back. But you don't have to take it. If you want to do this, then you knock yourself out."

Tara's heart thumped. Bastard. Absolute bastard. What the hell was his problem?

She took a deep breath.

And she knew there was only one thing she could do.

Call his fucking bluff.

"You know what?" Tara said. "I'll do that."

Sam's eyes widened.

Ha. Wasn't expecting that, was he?

She turned around, and she walked over towards that block of flats.

Over towards those muffled cries.

"I—I can hear you out there. Help me. Please. There's— there's nobody else here. I need... I need some help. Please."

She got closer down the path towards the block of flats, not looking back at Sam once. The flats weren't massive. Around four stories high. Well-kept grounds. Looked like some sort of assisted living setup, come to think of it.

She reached the front door and saw the glass was completely smashed.

She stood there.

Looked inside the darkness.

Listened to the birds singing.

Listened to the rain against the trees.

And something made her feel anxious about all this.

Something made her feel nervous about stepping inside.

Nervous about what she might find.

Something didn't feel... right.

She tensed her fists.

And then she stepped inside.

"Here goes nothing..."

She stepped inside the block of flats.

Through the smashed glass on the automatic doors.

She crunched her way through the glass. Further into the darkness. It was *so* dark in here.

And it was so quiet, too.

Too quiet.

She walked down the corridor.

Every footstep echoing.

The sound of her own shaky breathing the loudest thing she could hear.

Up ahead, she saw doors. Doors to rooms. Lots of doors.

Some of them were closed.

But most of them were open.

Like everyone had just got up and left this place.

What the hell had happened here?

Her heart raced.

She took another step.

"Hello?" she said.

Her voice echoed further down the corridors.

She went to step forward when suddenly she heard something above.

Footsteps.

Creaking along the floorboards.

Fear gripped her.

She looked up at the ceiling.

There was somebody up there.

But whoever was screaming for help...

There was no sign of them anymore.

She waited.

And then she climbed the stairs.

Slowly.

Quietly.

One step at a time.

She reached the top of the stairs, and she stopped.

More of those open doors.

And more of that *silence*.

An unwavering sense that this place had been abandoned.

That something had happened here.

She stood there, looking down the corridor. At the end, she saw a window with torn red curtains. She could smell something sour in the air. Something... *off*. A chill breeze swept over her, making her shiver.

She went to take another step when she heard a bang to her left.

A heavy bang.

An echo.

She jumped.

Fear grew inside her even more.

She looked around.

Looked for the source of that bang in the darkness.

But she didn't see anything.

She turned back to the corridor when suddenly she saw something up ahead on the floor. A bunch of leaflets sitting in a pile in front of the first door.

She walked up to them.

Crouched down.

Picked them up.

And when she looked at it, things started making sense.

They were leaflets from a construction company.

Eviction notices.

A final warning to vacate the premises before police involvement because they were about to demolish the building.

Tara looked at this pile of letters, then at the empty rooms, and then she saw the mess of shit, food, and trash some of the people had left here, and it suddenly all clicked into place.

The reason this place seemed abandoned was because it *was* abandoned.

Apart from...

That bang again.

Scratching.

And then: "Help!"

Tara spun around and saw someone standing right there on the stairs.

A dark silhouette.

Staring right at her.

Butterflies fluttered around her stomach.

Her knees went weak.

She needed to get away from here.

She needed...

And then she realised who it was.

"Sam," she said.

Sam walked towards her, Harvey by his side. "One person," he said. "Just one frigging person, okay? I'm not turning this into some pied piper charity cause."

A weight lifted from her shoulders. She had to admit she was happy to see him.

But she was still freaked out.

Because she didn't know where that muffled cry was coming from.

"It'd be good to help them out," Tara said. "If I knew where the hell they were."

Sam looked around, too. Scanned those open doors. "Well, have you checked every floor?"

"God, give me a minute, will you?"

"It's just..."

"Help! I'm—I'm in the lift. I'm in the lift!"

Tara froze.

She looked at Sam.

And he looked back at her.

"The lift," they both said in unison.

And then Tara saw it.

The lift doors.

Metal.

Solid.

And shut tight.

She walked over towards those doors.

Put a hand against the cold metal surface.

"Hello?" she said. "Is someone—is someone in there?"

Silence.

For a moment, silence.

And then: "I'm stuck. I—I can't get out. Help me. Help me, please. Don't—don't leave me here!"

Tara looked around at Sam.

Sam looked back at her.

He didn't have to say anything.

Because she knew it herself.

This man was stuck in a frigging elevator.

Stuck in a frigging elevator while there was no frigging power.

"Well," Sam said, finally breaking his silence. "You picked a bloody awkward one to rescue."

CHAPTER THIRTY-THREE

Sam stood in front of the elevator and listened to the man banging on the metal doors in there, and a part of him wished he'd just followed his instincts and kept on walking alone after all.

He could hear the man scratching against the metal doors like he was worried Sam and Tara had walked away and abandoned him. Every now and then, he shouted something like, "you still there?" To which Tara reassured him they were, every single time.

And Sam had to admit, being trapped in a lift in the middle of a bloody blackout was an awful predicament.

It was pretty much a death sentence. Especially since this place was pretty remote—and since it seemed like the rest of the block had done one before demolition day.

If he and Tara hadn't walked past and heard his cries, this place might well have become his tomb.

It might *still* be his tomb.

And Sam didn't want that on his conscience.

Nobody wanted that on their conscience.

And besides.

Sam had enough on his conscience...

Tara looked around at him, horror in her eyes. "What... what do we do here?"

Sam shrugged. "I thought you were the genius hell-bent on saving this guy?"

"Don't be a dick, mate. Forgive me for wanting to save someone begging for their fucking life, jeez."

She had a point.

They couldn't just walk away from this place without at least *trying* to help this man trapped inside.

It wasn't going to be easy. And there were no guarantees it was going to work.

But they had to try something.

Sam sighed. "I can't believe I'm actually bloody doing this..."

And then he stepped forward, up to the lift doors.

He grabbed the indentations between the doors.

Tried to stick his fingers in there, tried to prise them apart. If he could get some leverage, it wouldn't be too hard.

But he couldn't get any leverage.

He couldn't get his fingers in there at all.

"Any luck?" Tara asked.

Sam gritted his teeth. "Does it look like I'm having much luck?"

"Alright, sausage fingers. I was just asking."

"Well, don't. I really could do without stupid questions right now."

Tara shook her head. "You know, you're more of an arsehole than I first thought."

"First impressions count for shit."

"I'm clearly a terrible judge of character. Where's your bloody dental floss now when you really need something useful?"

Sam let go of the doors. He took a deep breath. If he could just get a little leverage, then he had a chance.

A chance of opening these doors.

A small chance, sure. But a chance all the same.

And that might be the difference between this man living or dying.

"Are you—are you still there?" the man in the lift shouted.

Sam rolled his eyes. "Yes. Still here."

"And not going anywhere until we get you out of there," Tara added.

Sam glared at her. No way were they staying around here much longer. If they couldn't get him out, then they were just gonna have to walk away and give up. They'd tried. Their conscience was clear.

Or... well.

A little clearer.

His conscience would never be totally clear.

He stepped forward again and pushed his fingertips into that crevice between the doors as hard as he could.

Tried to stuff his fingers in.

Tried for a little leverage.

For just a little...

And then he saw her in his mind's eye.

Covered in blood.

Wide eyes staring out at him through that smoked-out window.

Please don't leave me. Please! Help me!

He saw her.

And he saw the rest of them.

All of them staring out at him.

All of them banging on the glass.

All of them begging for his help...

He saw them all, and he felt his heart racing, and he felt his chest tightening, and he knew he needed to get away.

He knew he needed to push the memory away.

He knew—

"Hey."

A voice.

Right beside him.

Tara.

She looked at him with wide eyes.

Like she was concerned.

Like she could see he was losing his shit right now.

Sam opened his mouth to explain he couldn't get into the elevator. He just couldn't do it.

But then she lifted something. Held it out to him. "This help?"

She was holding a long piece of metal.

It didn't look the strongest in the world.

But it *might* fit between that crack in the elevator doors.

It just might.

He nodded at her.

Took it from her.

And then he walked back over to the elevator doors.

"You hold on in there," he said. "We're coming for you."

He stuck the top end of that long piece of metal between the crevices in the lift door.

It slotted right in. Just about fitting.

He felt a glimmer of relief.

This might work.

This might actually work.

He closed his eyes.

And he saw them in his mind's eye again.

He saw them begging.

He heard them screaming.

And he felt so helpless, and so lost, and so…

He pushed.

Pushed hard against that piece of metal wedged in the elevator doors.

"Come on," he said.

He pushed even harder.

The doors weren't budging.

But he had some leverage.

He had some leverage, and that was all he needed.

"Are you—are you still there?" the man called.

"Yes," Sam shouted through gritted teeth. "Still here."

He saw Rebecca, then.

Saw her sitting there in front of him.

Tears streaming down her cheeks.

"I'm afraid, Sam. I'm worried about you. You need some therapy. You need some help. But I... I can't stay here and watch you turn into what you're turning into..."

He felt the stinging pain of those words—words he would never forget, words that had changed the course of his life forever—and he pushed even harder against that piece of metal.

And then he felt it.

The elevator doors shifting open.

Adrenaline kicked in.

He'd done it.

He'd opened those doors, and he'd actually done it.

A smile stretched up his face.

He looked at Tara.

"I..."

And then he saw something.

The look in her eyes.

It wasn't a look of delight.

It was a look of...

Shock?

Sam turned to the elevator doors to see what she was so shocked about when he saw it, right away.

There was total darkness through those elevator doors.

But it wasn't the darkness of the elevator itself.

It was the darkness of the elevator shaft.

"What..." Sam started.

And then it clicked.

He stared into that darkness, and in one horrifying realisation, it clicked.

"He's... he's on another floor," Tara said. Echoing Sam's thoughts exactly.

Sam's heart thudded.

He stared into that darkness, totally still.

No idea what to do.

No idea how to progress.

Just even more sure of something.

They weren't getting this man out of here.

"Are you—are you still there?" the man called. His voice quite clearly above, now. "What's—what's happening? I heard summat. Where are you?"

Sam opened his dry mouth and went to say something. He didn't know what to say. But he knew he needed to say *something*.

"We... we might have a problem," he started.

"Problem?" the man said. "What—oh, shit. Oh, shit, shit, shit."

Above, the elevator started to creak.

He heard wires snapping.

"Shit! I'm falling! I'm fucking falling!"

And as Sam stood there in front of that open door, all he could do was listen.

All he could do was watch.

"What—" Tara started.

She didn't finish.

Because the elevator hurtled past them and went crashing towards the floor.

The man wasn't screaming anymore.

CHAPTER THIRTY-FOUR

Tara waited for a sign of life from the man who'd just hurtled down the elevator shaft.

But the more time passed, and the more the silence stretched on, she felt her hopes weren't going to be granted.

She stood at the elevator door that Sam had just prized open, totally frozen. She couldn't believe what she'd just witnessed.

The elevator, tumbling down the shaft.

Crashing to the ground with an immense explosion below.

The man inside it going from screaming to silence, all in an instant.

And as she stood there, Sam and Harvey right beside her, she knew she would have to go downstairs soon. She knew she was going to have to investigate.

She knew she would have to see what was left of the man.

She knew she would have to see his fate for herself.

She turned around.

Saw Sam staring.

Transfixed.

He looked lost. He'd looked like this a few times now. Like he was lost in a memory. Haunted by something from his past.

She looked at him, and she wanted to ask if he was okay.

She wanted to tell him there was nothing else he could've done.

That this wasn't his fault.

Because she knew the look in his eyes.

She recognised guilt when she saw it.

She wanted to comfort him.

She wanted to reassure him.

But she saw that elevator shaft, and she knew she needed to get downstairs.

Get to that man.

Find out what sort of state he was in.

Fast.

"I... I'll see you down there," Tara said.

Sam didn't respond.

He just stood there.

Eyes wide.

And for a moment, as she looked at his completely focused, completely transfixed face, she swore she saw tears.

She turned around and walked down the stairs.

Dread followed her every step.

Dread over what she might encounter.

Dread over what she might find.

She kept on going.

Walking, step by step towards the remains at the bottom of the elevator shaft.

Still no sounds.

Still no screams.

Still fearing the absolute worst.

She reached the ground floor, and she stopped, right there. Turned around. Looked back up those stairs.

Sam was still standing there.

Still transfixed by something.

Still caught in a memory, quite clearly.

Caught in trauma.

She felt sorry for him. As much as an arse as he'd been with her... she sensed there was more to his actions and the way he was than he was letting on.

Or maybe she was just being blinded by the fact she was quite... *interested* in him.

But fuck. There'd be a time to psychoanalyse the shit out of him.

And that time wasn't now.

She turned back around.

Walked down the last few steps.

And then she turned around to face the elevator.

The door was twisted and bent. It was still partly open, still ajar.

And she could see the remains of the elevator inside it.

Her heart started racing.

She pictured all kinds of horrors.

All kinds of awful things.

She pictured masses of blood.

She pictured twisted bones.

She pictured a cracked skull with brain spilling out.

And then she pictured it was Jonno lying there, and as horrid as it made her feel—as guilty as it made her feel—imagining it was him lying there made her feel better.

She tightened her fists.

And then she walked over towards that elevator.

There was no movement inside the elevator. And there were still no sounds inside the elevator. And she was pretty sure she could see something else inside that elevator now.

Blood.

She gulped.

Took another step towards the elevator.

Grabbed the doors.

Started to slide them open.

And that's when she heard it.

"I... You're here. You... you found me."

Tara froze.

Confusion.

Shock.

But mostly...

Elation.

Because that voice.

That voice was coming from inside the elevator.

It was coming from right in front of her.

She stepped forward another step. Squinted into the darkness.

And then she saw him.

Sitting right there on the floor of the elevator in front of her, there was a man.

He looked like he was around sixty. Long grey beard. Thin. And he had a few scrapes and bruises.

But he was alive.

He was actually alive.

A smile stretched across Tara's face. She couldn't help herself. Couldn't suppress it.

"Come on," she said, pushing against the doors with as much force as she could. "Let's—let's help get you out of here."

She pushed as hard as she could. And then the man stood up and pushed along with her, too.

They both pushed, and Tara felt elation. She felt hope.

They pushed until the doors creaked open, and the man stepped out.

He stood there in front of her. Tears streaming down his face. A smile cracking the corners of his mouth.

And then he grabbed her hands with his shaky hands and got to his knees.

"Thank you," he said. "Thank you for not leaving me. Thank you for coming here for me. For helping me. Bless you. God bless you."

Tara smiled as this man crouched there on his knees, sobbing away, so, so grateful.

She heard a creaking noise behind her.

Saw Sam standing there.

She smiled at him.

He looked at her with wide eyes, and she nodded back at him. Half-smiled.

She could tell he was happy.

She could tell he was relieved.

But at the same time, she could see something else in Sam's eyes.

Trauma.

CHAPTER THIRTY-FIVE

As much as Sam wanted to get home as soon as possible, he was beginning to lose hope that they'd make it back before sunset.

It was already getting dark. Which was crazy because it meant they'd been travelling far longer than he realised. Today had absolutely vanished in a haze before his very eyes. He couldn't believe that it was only earlier today that he was fighting his way into the city centre, being thrown out of his car by the brute whose girlfriend he'd ended up helping and travelling back with

Yeah. It'd been a long day.

A hell of a day.

He wanted to keep on going. Wanted to keep pressing on. Especially after the incident with the man, Franco, in the elevator, too. What a shitshow that'd been. They'd tried saving the bloke, then they'd thought they'd lost the bloke, and then when they'd saved the bloke, it turned out the bloke wanted to do his own thing anyway and ignore all their advice about not heading back into the city...

Yeah. At least they'd given him another chance.

But people were going to be hard to get through to in these

times of crisis.

That was just something he had to accept.

Something they all had to accept.

He felt a whole combination of emotions about what happened in there. The whole sorry cascade.

Relief.

But also...

The memory.

He saw the memory.

The memory of Iraq.

And the memory of Rebecca.

He was seeing these memories so frequently now that he wasn't sure he could suppress them for much longer.

He was in a more industrial area now. Lots of industrial units about. A sorting office, which was absolutely rammed full of post vans. He could see workers sitting there, smoking away on their cigarettes, waiting for some kind of answer, some kind of hope. Just a little back, he'd seen the remains of a nasty lorry accident. A woman, impaled in her seat. Little baby in the back of the car splattered in blood. They were trying to get the baby out and remove the mother's body, too.

So many tragedies.

And so many tragedies they hadn't even witnessed yet.

He looked around, and he caught Tara looking at him.

She was a funny one. Always seemed to be looking at him. And then, when he looked at her, she'd glance away, pretend her attention was elsewhere.

And he knew she was looking at him. He wasn't stupid.

He knew she was judging him for the way he'd frozen at the elevator.

And he knew she wasn't the sort of woman who was going to be able to hold off asking questions for too long.

Hell. He couldn't blame her. Especially with some of the shit she'd been through.

He walked further down this street, and he felt his legs and ankles aching. His feet were soggy and frozen solid. By his current estimations and going by this current route—not the quickest, but the best option he had right now not only to try and avoid the worst of the storm, but also the biggest pockets of people—they were still a good few hours off his place.

A good few hours that could get ugly.

He didn't fancy the idea of sheltering out here. But he was beginning to wonder if they had a choice. The rain was getting heavier. The storm was really picking up. They'd been walking a long time, and it really didn't feel so safe anymore.

"We should rest up a little," Tara said.

Sam turned around to her. And then he looked at Harvey. Even he was looking a bit knackered. Which was pretty unheard of for this dog with boundless energy. "*We?*"

"Well," Tara said. "You can do what you want. But I'm starting to think you're quite fond of having me around."

Sam smirked. "You think so, do you?"

"I'd say you could have walked away when we were at the flats earlier. And... I don't know. Something about you tells me you like company more than you're letting on."

He didn't like how accurate she was. He didn't like how *right* she was.

But she was right. He did like her company. He was beginning to enjoy it a lot.

And it felt weird, feeling that way over someone he'd barely known a few hours. And someone who he was pretty sure was going to wander out of his life in no time at all.

There was something about her that made him feel... comfortable.

And that felt dangerous.

He knew what happened when he got comfortable around people.

He lowered his head. "Look. I... I was thinking. And you're

probably right. We should find somewhere. Rest up. Even just for a few hours. I know Harvey here won't forgive me if we end up walking much further."

Tara smiled. "Told you, you're fond of having me around."

"It's purely practical," he said. "Don't flatter yourself."

They found an old electricity substation right in the thick of the woods behind an old cycle path, which people were still whizzing past. It was made from brick and had metal barriers around it, which would give them an extra layer of security—if they needed it.

"You really know how to treat a lady, don't you?" Tara said.

Sam pulled the cobweb-laden door open. Spiders crawled around, scurrying everywhere. It smelled damp inside, which probably wasn't good for an old electricity substation. But it was roomy enough for them to shelter in. "As long as the power doesn't suddenly spark back online, I think we'll be good. We'll set up a tent inside so we're even more sheltered. Come on."

They set up the tent together, sat there in the rain, and didn't speak. They took their shoes off, which was a major relief after the day they'd had. They ate some peanut butter crackers between them. They were both exhausted and pretty starving, that was for sure. But Sam didn't feel like he could eat much, and neither did Tara, apparently. Must be the adrenaline.

Neither of them spoke. They just watched the heavens open, watched that rain pour from the darkening sky above, a little fire crackling right in front of them.

Every now and then, Sam looked at Tara. And he always saw her looking back at him.

"You got something to say?" he asked.

"I guess... I guess I wanted to thank you."

"You've thanked me enough already—"

"I know it can't have been easy. Stepping in when you did. And... and it's pretty clear this whole journey's not been easy for you. For whatever reason. Really, that's none of my business. But

I... I guess I just want you to know I appreciate it. I appreciate you letting me come along with you. No matter what happens next."

He looked into her eyes, and he felt his stomach flutter.

"Well," Sam said. "I've kind of liked having you around, too."

"You have a funny way of showing it."

Sam smirked. "Yeah. I've heard that before."

He looked off into the fire. Started into those burning embers.

"My ex-wife," he said. "Rebecca. We used to go wild camping a lot. Just pack our bags and set off and end up wherever the hell we ended up. Sometimes the Lake District. Sometimes Scotland. Sometimes even France. We'd sit in front of the fire, and we'd just stare at the flames and the stars, not saying a word. Sometimes for hours. But it just felt... perfect, you know? Like we were the only two people in the whole world."

Tara smiled. She lowered her head. "Believe it or not, Jonno used to be relatively romantic. Before I realised he was a walking red flag, anyway."

"You didn't realise *he* was a walking red flag?"

"People can be deceiving at first sight."

Sam nodded. "Yeah. Yeah, I suppose they can."

More eye contact.

Time dragging on even longer as they looked into one another's eyes.

As the flames reflected in Tara's eyes, making them glow.

"What happened to her?" Tara asked.

"What?"

"Your... your ex-wife. Rebecca. Is she..."

She didn't want to finish. Out of politeness, it seemed.

But Sam felt a little gazumped by the question even though he should've seen it coming.

He thought about coming up with some sort of explanation. Some sort of excuse. Some sort of way of burying his head in the sand like he'd always done.

But maybe this was the moment that changed.

Maybe this was the moment things were going to start being different.

He looked back into the flickering flames. "She's not dead. If that's what you're wondering."

"That's... that's a relief."

"She left me four years ago. Because... because of something I went through. Something I tried to... something I tried to run from. But something I... something I'm not sure I can run from much longer."

He looked at Tara. Glanced at her for just a second.

She sat there.

Waiting for him.

Waiting for him to say whatever he needed to say.

"And I... I see now that it was right. What she did. Walking away. Because... because I see now what I was doing to myself. What I'd become. But I... It's hard. When you've been through something. When you've... when you've seen the things I've seen. It's hard."

Tara stayed silent.

Waiting.

Listening.

Not asking.

Not prying.

Just listening.

And he appreciated that.

He felt comfortable with that.

He felt like he'd felt with Rebecca about that.

"Maybe... maybe one day, when all this blows over, I'll tell you what I went through. I'll tell you everything. But not now. This alone... this alone is a big step. And I still can't quite bloody believe I'm pouring my heart out to a woman I've barely known a day. But life's weird like that, isn't it?"

He looked into Tara's eyes, and he saw her smile.

"Life is weird," she said.

They stared at each other a little longer.

That tension growing between them.

That warmth growing between them.

"We should get some sleep," Sam said. "Even if it's just an hour."

Tara nodded. Opened her mouth like she was going to say something else. Then twiddled this bracelet she wore around nervously.

And then she just closed it and smiled. "Yeah," she said. "Yeah, we should."

He had a sudden urge to go over there and wrap an arm around her.

But instead, he threw her a sleeping bag and made it somewhat comfortable for her, under the extra shelter of the tent from out of his bug-out bag.

And then he smiled and nodded at her, and he walked into the back of this damp, dreary cabin.

He lay on his back and listened to the flames flickering away, to the rain pouring down, and he felt a cool breeze creep inside the electricity substation.

When he looked around, he saw Tara staring at him.

Only this time, she didn't look away.

She smiled at him.

Nodded at him.

And then she closed her eyes.

He lay there and stared at her lying there, and he felt comfortable.

He felt safe

He felt more himself than he'd felt in a long time.

Happier than he'd felt in a long time.

He closed his eyes, and he took a deep breath of the cool night air.

And in the midst of crisis, a smile crept across Sam's face.

CHAPTER THIRTY-SIX

Jonno stared into the darkness at Tara and her new fuckbuddy getting all cosy in that electricity substation, and he felt like he wanted to be sick.

It was late. Dark now. The rain hammered down from above. Lightning flashed every now and then, illuminating the sky momentarily with a burst of light.

And it made Jonno rather conscious. Conscious that one of them might look over here and see him. Conscious that that dog might notice him and start barking at him.

But then he smiled as he stood sodden in the pouring rain.

He felt invisible.

Truly invisible.

They weren't noticing him.

Nobody was noticing him.

He stared at where he knew Tara and that bastard had disappeared to. Stared into the darkness they'd retreated towards after sitting so cosy around that fire. He'd seen how Tara looked at the man. Seen the way she looked into his eyes. There was a curiosity there. A warmth there. And as much as Jonno was convinced Tara *must* have been fucking this man behind his back... he started to wonder if it even mattered at all.

The only thing that seemed to matter right now was that Tara had run away from him.

No. Not only that.

She'd embarrassed him.

She'd humiliated him.

She'd left him for dead.

And now, here she was, smirking away in the presence of another man.

Slut.

Absolute fucking ugly slut.

He swallowed a lump in his throat. He could taste vomit. Vomit and blood. His head ached, too. Splitting pain, really bad. He kept on scratching it and sending a shooting bolt of agony right down his neck, right down his spine. She'd hit him good with that wine bottle. Real good.

And if these were normal times—if the power hadn't gone out—he'd probably be in a hospital somewhere right now. Probably even having scans on his head to check there wasn't too much damage or that nothing serious was happening to him.

But these weren't normal times.

He tensed his fists as he stared into that darkness and felt a burning sense of anger. A volcano of anger bubbling right up to the surface. Tara had not only humiliated him. She'd not only thrown all the good he'd done for her over the years right back into his face. But she'd had the absolute audacity to move on, so quickly, while he was out here in the rain.

Well, it wasn't on.

And he wasn't standing for it.

He gritted his teeth, and he pictured her lying in a pool of blood.

He imagined her new prick of a boyfriend lying by her side, throat slit.

He imagined the dog whining as he buried a blade deep between its ribs, time and time again.

And he smiled.

He was going to have fun with them.

A lot of fun.

He took a deep breath, and he crept down closer towards the electricity substation.

It was time for him to get started.

CHAPTER THIRTY-SEVEN

Tara jolted awake and gasped with fear.

She was outside somewhere. In the darkness. And for a moment, before she properly got her bearings or acclimated to her sense of self, she was convinced that Jonno had done something to her. That he'd tied her up. Thrown her in some sort of dark cellar somewhere, and that she was trapped.

She was trapped, and she wasn't getting out.

But then she looked around, and she realised exactly where she was.

It was raining outside. Not as heavily as it was earlier. She was in some kind of shelter. An old electricity substation. She took a deep breath of the cool air as she stared out at that sky, filled with flashes from lightning, and felt a combination of emotions.

Fear. Pure terror. Because she was stuck out here in the middle of the night in the pouring rain, and she wanted to be back at home. She wanted to be tucked up in bed; she wanted to be far away from here.

But also…

Also, she felt a sense of freedom.

A sense of freedom she hadn't felt in a long time.

Because she was far away from home.

She was far away from Jonno.

And for another reason, too.

She looked around, and she saw Sam lying there.

His eyes were closed. His chest was rising and falling slowly. He was sleeping.

And he looked comfortable. He looked relaxed. He looked at peace. More at peace than anyone probably should look in a world where the power had just gone out.

And Tara didn't know what tomorrow would bring. She didn't know whether Sam's fears about these blackouts were going to wind up true. She didn't know whether the power was really going to be out for as long as he said. She didn't know whether he was just being melodramatic or not.

But she knew one thing.

Much as she hated to admit it… she felt safe in his company.

She felt like there were no flies on him.

She felt like she had nothing to worry about with him.

She looked over at him and felt a little flutter in her chest.

She knew it was wrong. After all, she'd only just left Jonno.

But had she really?

She'd mentally checked out of that relationship a long time ago. So was it really so wrong that she was feeling this way about someone else now?

And why did she always feel like she had to be reliant on someone else?

Why did she always feel the need for connection?

She lay there and stared at Sam, stared at Harvey lying beside him, and she wondered. She thought about what he'd told her. About how he'd gone through something. How his ex, Rebecca, left him four years ago because of something that happened to him.

And how he said he'd tell her one day.

She wanted to know what hid beneath the surface.

She wanted to know it all.

But she knew she needed to be patient.

Sam deserved patience right now.

Where trauma was concerned, everyone deserved patience.

She looked over at Sam, and she thought about what her parents would say, and she felt a knot in her stomach.

Because she knew what they'd say.

That she was leaning on someone else.

Or that she needed to find her own two feet rather than relying on someone else.

Or that he was too good for her, or too bad for her, or something in between.

She thought about what they would say, and for a moment, just a moment, she wondered why she took their opinions so seriously, and whether she even wanted to go home at all.

Maybe there was another way.

Maybe Sam was her other way.

She was about to keep on mulling this conundrum over when she saw movement just outside the electricity substation.

She froze. Squinted out into the dark.

She'd seen someone.

Someone walking by.

She didn't know why she felt so weird about it. It wasn't like people had vanished or anything. At the end of the day, there were bound to be people lurking around at night, searching for shelter.

But at the same time...

She didn't realise just how on display they were in here.

How sheltered she'd felt earlier and how in the open she felt now.

She needed to get up and close those doors. She didn't like the thought that people could be out there, looking in, watching her sleep.

She got up. Crept across the cold, damp concrete floor and

over to the doors. Being extra careful to try not to wake Sam or Harvey up.

She climbed over the top of them and looked down.

Looked at Harvey, lying there right by Sam's side.

Sam's arm around him.

And it looked sweet. Seeing the pair of them so close like this.

Sam clearly cared about this dog. Clearly loved him very much.

She smiled. And then she looked around and started to walk towards the metal doors again.

That's when she saw something that made her heart skip a beat.

The little gate up ahead.

It was open.

They hadn't left it open. She was sure they hadn't left it open.

And yet...

She looked back at Sam.

Thought about waking him. About warning him.

But then, how pathetic did that make her look?

She needed to show a bit of self-reliance.

She needed to show a bit of common sense.

She needed to show her strength.

Even if just to herself.

She walked to that gate.

Reached out to grab it, to pull it shut.

And that's when she saw it.

The hand.

Appearing out of nowhere.

Grabbing her arm.

She froze.

Went to call out.

But it was already too late.

Someone had hold of her.

Had their sweaty hand around her mouth.

Dragged her out of that gate, with nothing she could do about it.

She felt the hand pressing against her face.

She felt hot breath on her neck.

And then she heard a little chuckle.

"Hello, princess," Jonno said. "Fancy seeing you here."

CHAPTER THIRTY-EIGHT

Sam opened his eyes, and for the first time in as long as he could remember, he felt at peace.

It was light. And he couldn't hear the rain anymore. Smelled like the morning after a storm. The beautiful scent of "petrichor," as it was called. Rebecca always reminded him that's what it was called, all the damned time. He used to pretend to forget because it irritated her in that cute way that irritating the person you love always is.

But he never forgot.

And he never would forget.

He thought about her right now. Wondered where she was. And wondered if she'd be sitting there thinking, shit. Sam was right about all this crap.

He wondered if she ever even thought about him at all.

And then he thought about Tara. He lay there and saw the light peeking through the open door, and he smiled. He could hear birds singing out there, a sound that always calmed him, always comforted him. It was strange how silent everything else was, though. Usually, didn't matter where you were in Preston, you'd hear the buzz of traffic somewhere in the distance, whether it was the main road or the motorway.

So that sealed it, then.

That made him realise that this power outage, this blackout, was serious.

That it was still a thing.

And that made him worry a little.

Because he knew how people would respond and react when they found out the power was still out.

He felt that little knot of tension in his stomach.

He just had to get back home.

He didn't have much further to go now.

And once he got back there… well. That's when his survival skills were really going to be put to the test.

He thought about how hungry he was. How much he wanted breakfast and how ready for that he was.

And then he thought about Tara. All he had to teach her. All she had to learn.

He thought about them going hunting together this morning. Thought about teaching her how to set up different sorts of traps. Reverse snare traps to catch smaller animals. How to skin animals, and how to preserve the meat. And the thought didn't fill him with the sort of fear it would no doubt fill most people.

Instead, it sparked a strange kind of optimism.

A strange kind of happiness.

He turned over and saw Harvey sitting there, head on his paws, staring out into the light.

"What you looking at me like that for, eh?" he asked. "You used to have it far worse, lad."

And that was true. Harvey was a rescue dog. He came from a pretty rough background. Used to get neglected and kicked by his owner, apparently. Made him really cautious of people at first, men especially.

Building his trust had taken a lot of time and effort, but they'd got there in the end.

And now... now, it was like Sam was the only person Harvey could truly trust.

So the fact he'd taken to Tara so quickly said a lot about her.

He rolled over onto his other side to where he knew Tara had fallen asleep, and then he noticed something.

She wasn't there.

She was gone.

He sat up. Frowned. "Where..."

But there was no point saying anything.

There was no point saying anything at all.

Because she wasn't here.

He got up. Walked over to the substation opening. Looked outside, into the light.

The streets were empty. Still the same couple of cars sitting there, most of them vacant and abandoned now. Further up the street, where the area got more suburban, he swore he could hear distant voices. Distant screams? He couldn't be sure.

He stood there, and he looked around. Maybe she'd just gone out for something. Or maybe she was just out for a morning walk. Or perhaps even she'd decided to get a head start and go find something they could eat for breakfast herself.

But the more Sam stood there, and the more he thought about it, the more his sense of sadness and acceptance began to grow.

Because it didn't matter what he thought. And it didn't matter what he speculated.

Tara was gone.

CHAPTER THIRTY-NINE

Sam wasn't sure how long he stood outside the electricity substation, but he couldn't wrap his head around the feelings and emotions he was experiencing.

He stood there as the morning sun shone down from above. He could see water pooling down the roads, but not as much as yesterday. He could see the road back towards the city up ahead. And just seeing that road made him feel nervous. The thought of going back to the city today. The thought of going back that way when he knew just how bad things would be getting, how rapidly things would be deteriorating.

He knew he needed to get far away from this place. Because the suburbs weren't going to be much better as time progressed. There would be looting, and there would be vulgarity. The longer this crisis went on, the more violence would spread from the inner cities and beyond.

He needed to get back home. He lived in a more rural area outside of town. Wasn't exactly countryside, but it was close.

He couldn't afford to stick around here. He couldn't afford to twiddle his thumbs.

But it was Tara he kept on thinking of.

He thought of the conversation they'd had last night. How close he'd come to opening up to her. And that hurt. It hurt because... because he shouldn't have done that. He shouldn't have got so close like that. He shouldn't have grown vulnerable like that.

He was a fool for ever thinking she might be someone he could open up to.

Someone he could be comfortable with.

He shook his head. He was an idiot. An idiot for ever thinking there could be something there between them.

An idiot for seeing something in her.

Because he barely knew her.

And even worse than that... *she* barely knew *him*.

She wouldn't be so interested if she knew his past.

Maybe that's why it was. Maybe she'd sensed it. Maybe he'd already opened up a little bit too much last night, and he'd misread things, and she wasn't as comfortable with him as he wanted her to be.

He looked down the road, and he felt a sinking feeling in his stomach. Because he couldn't deny that when he'd woken up, he'd felt this ... longing.

He'd felt this anticipation.

This excitement.

He was looking forward to seeing her.

He was looking forward to chatting to her. To the day ahead.

He was looking forward to getting to know her more.

And he didn't know what the rest of the day had in store. He didn't have a clue what the rest of his and Tara's friendship had in store—if he could call it a friendship.

But... he was looking forward to this morning.

He was looking forward to seeing her again.

And now she was gone.

He stood there, and he took a deep breath. The abandonment. The same sense of abandonment he'd felt when Rebecca left.

He was at his weakest.

His lowest.

And she'd walked tearfully out of the door and left.

And he knew he couldn't feel any anger towards her. He understood. After all, she'd put up with far more than most women could've done.

But he'd never forget that moment and how he'd felt.

The sense of sadness he'd felt.

The sense of his whole world being torn away from him.

And that sense that his demons were finally catching up with him—as much as he'd tried to outrun them, and as much as he'd tried to escape them.

They'd caught up with him. Of course, they'd caught up with him.

Just like he always knew they would.

And here he was, staring down this slope and facing the same sort of inevitability.

The same sort of realisation.

Tara was gone.

She'd walked away.

For whatever reason, she'd decided to walk away.

He didn't need to know why.

He never would know why.

He was on his own again.

And that was what he wanted, really, wasn't it?

He stood there, Harvey panting by his side, and he felt the powerful, tight knot of loneliness tightening even more.

"Come on, Harvey," he said. "Let's…"

And then he stopped.

He stopped because he saw something right there on the road in front of him.

He crouched down.

Picked it up.

And when he saw it, when it clicked, his stomach sank.

Because in his hand, he saw a silver bracelet.

A bracelet Tara had worn.

There, snapped, in his palm.

CHAPTER FORTY

Sam stood with the torn bracelet in his hand, and he wasn't sure how to feel.

The sun was bright and warm. The flooding was bad, but the weather was alright now, which went against all the fear-mongering they'd been doing on the news. So they *were* being melodramatic, as predicted.

But that said... the rain had been bad. And the floods were bad.

And coupled with the blackout, a lot of chaos had been caused, and a lot of damage had been done.

But as he stood in the middle of the road, he felt anxious. He felt nervous.

And he felt torn.

Because this bracelet.

Tara.

What it meant.

He stood there, and he held the bracelet in his hand. He didn't know what it meant. Well... it was an expensive bracelet. And it wasn't the sort of bracelet you'd just snap off your wrist and then leave right here in a hurry.

Although... he didn't know that. Not for certain. It could've been a bracelet that psycho ex-boyfriend of hers got her. She could've been eager to shed herself of all her old ties, and that was just a part of it.

It was possible. A definite possibility.

But... he just wasn't sure.

Something didn't feel right.

Something didn't feel right at all.

He looked down at the bracelet. And then he looked at the road back towards the city. He knew it wasn't going to be a good journey to take. He knew it was going to be a dangerous road. He knew he was going to come across all kinds of things he didn't want to. He was going to come across panic, and he was going to come across chaos, and he was going to come across confusion.

And for what?

For a woman he barely knew?

For a woman who wasn't even his responsibility?

For a stranger?

Risk everything for *that*?

He looked over his shoulder. Back towards the road home. He could be there well before sunset. He could hunt for himself. He could be home, and he could be sheltered, and he could be out of the way of all this crap—and well set to survive in this world.

Well. Better set than anyone else he knew, anyway.

He stood there and looked back, and as much as he knew, logically, that heading home was the right decision, that heading home made sense...

He turned back around.

He felt butterflies in his stomach and in his chest.

He tightened his grip around the broken bracelet.

He thought about Rebecca's smile.

Then about the way Tara looked at him last night.

He knew it wasn't the sensible thing to do.

He knew it wasn't the logical thing to do.

But he knew it was the only thing he could do.
He was going back to the city.
He was going back for Tara.
He was going to find her.
Whatever it took.

CHAPTER FORTY-ONE

Tara stared into the darkness and wondered if she'd ever see light again.

It was pitch black, and she had absolutely no idea where she was. Her head hurt, bad. She couldn't remember why. Not properly.

All she remembered was Jonno.

Appearing out of nowhere.

Grabbing her.

Covering her mouth.

"Hello, princess. Fancy seeing you here."

And then dragging her off somewhere, away from that electricity substation, into the darkness.

She'd struggled. She'd tried to break free. Tried to kick out and tried to scratch at him. But he was just too strong.

And in the end, when he grew tired of her struggling, she couldn't pinpoint exactly when, but she'd felt a sharp, heavy pain crack against her head, and then the next thing she knew, she was cold, shivering, and enshrouded in darkness. Total darkness.

She tasted blood on her lips. Her wrists were bound tight

together, so tight it felt like the ties were digging into her skin. Her mouth was dry. She felt tired. Weak. Exhausted. Broken. She was blindfolded.

She had no idea where she was. What time it was.

And she had no idea where Jonno was, either.

And she felt afraid.

She felt pathetic for feeling afraid. She felt weak for wanting someone to help her. For wanting Mum and Dad to bail her out.

Or for wanting Sam to help her.

She thought of Sam, and her stomach turned even more. She pictured him chasing her. Racing after her. Trying to find her.

She pictured him desperately searching for her and then giving up when he realised he couldn't find her.

Or worse.

Waking up.

Seeing she was gone.

And not knowing why she'd gone. Thinking she'd just walked away. Thinking she'd just left.

She wished he was here.

She wished he was right here, wherever right here was.

But at the same time...

He wasn't. There was nobody here. Nobody who could help her.

Getting out of this place was on her. Completely on her.

So she had to figure out her own way out of here.

She had to do whatever she could to get out of here.

She had to fight.

She tried to snap the ties around her wrists. Tried to yank them apart as hard as she could.

But it just made the pain across her wrists even more intense.

Even sharper.

She closed her burning eyes. The blindfold around her head, covering her eyes, was so tight that it made her skull feel like it was going to crack under the force. She tried to stand, but she was tied around the waist, too. Tied to what? She wasn't sure. And she didn't hold out much hope that she'd be able to get out of the mess she was in.

But she'd be damned if she didn't try.

She tried to yank herself back to her feet when suddenly she heard a voice opposite her.

"You can try and get out as much as you like. It's not happening, sweetie."

When Tara heard that voice, every inch of her body went cold.

Because she knew to who that voice belonged.

She knew very well.

Shuffling.

Footsteps.

Walking over towards her.

Her body went numb. She felt cold. Like a rabbit in the headlights.

Her heart started racing faster and faster.

She felt anxiety taking a grip of her.

Taking control.

She'd told herself not to fear Jonno. Told herself all these years that as much as he intimidated her, it was his emotional abuse that was more dangerous than anything.

But now, she was beginning to question whether that was the case at all.

The footsteps stopped. And they stopped for long enough that she didn't know whether he was still there. Whether he was standing in front of her or not. Where he was at all.

She opened her mouth. Tried to speak. But she was gagged, too. Gagged and could taste her own saliva, and the blood on her lips, and vomit.

She sat there, helpless, and she thought of him standing opposite her.

Staring at her.

And she went cold.

Every inch of her body went cold.

She needed to get out of here.

She needed to get—

A pressure.

A pressure on the sides of her face.

Jonno dragging the blindfold away from her.

And then suddenly, in the darkness, she saw light.

She looked around. She didn't know where she was. Didn't recognise it. It looked like some sort of shed. A little garden shed. She could see it was light outside. Which meant she'd been here quite some time. Must've been passing in and out of consciousness, losing all track of the time.

She looked up at Jonno, and she saw the smirk on his face. She saw the bags under his eyes, heavy and blue. And she saw the speck of spit on his chin. He looked... demented. He looked *lost*.

He didn't look well.

Not one bit.

And that scared Tara even more.

She knew he could be emotionally irrational.

She knew he could be impulsive.

And she knew he could be dangerous now.

He looked down at her like she was dirt. Like she was a spider trapped in a glass. And he looked at her like he had a world of possibility in front of him. Like he had a ton of options.

He looked at her like he was mulling over what to do to her.

Thinking of all the awful things he might do to her.

"You really thought you'd get away so easily, didn't you?" Jonno said. "You really thought you'd be able to leave me, just like that. After all these years. Sweet, huh?"

She shook her head. Tried to speak. But that gag just blocked her speaking. She wondered where they were. Why nobody was nearby. If she could get this gag off, maybe she could call for help. Maybe...

No.

She wasn't always going to be able to call for help.

She wasn't always going to be able to rely on other people.

She had to help herself right now.

Jonno smirked. Shook his head. "I mean... excuse me. Excuse me for thinking four years counted for something. For something more than a crack across the head. And I know. I know. I was a bit... rough, back at the flat. But that's what you did to me. We could've just communicated. We could've talked it through. If you were having... problems with you and me, you could've told me, and we could've worked something out. Couldn't we?"

She wanted to tell him no. They couldn't. And even if she thought they could, there was absolutely no way he'd hear her out if she communicated with him.

And the very fact he thought this was on her—the very fact that he was trying to gaslight her into believing *she* was the problem—told her everything she needed to know about this monster.

Jonno sighed. Shook his head. "But, hey. Here we are. Reunited. Not the way I wanted, but you didn't make it easy for me. But you know what also isn't easy? What you did to me."

She saw the dried blood on his forehead, trickling from his sweaty hair, where she'd hit him with the wine bottle.

Where she'd smashed it right over his head.

"Attacking me. Leaving me for dead. And then... your little new boyfriend. Well."

He smiled, then. And he smiled with such a sinister expression that it filled Tara with fear.

Sam.

Had he done something to Sam?

Had he hurt him?

"I don't think we'll need to worry about him anymore," he said. "Or his dog."

Tara felt sick. He'd killed them. This monster had actually

killed them. He'd flipped, and he'd flipped on the day the emergency services had collapsed and law and order had failed.

He'd flipped, and he was going to get away with it.

He looked right into her eyes, which she felt streaming, and he puffed out his lips and smiled, shaking his head. "He's okay," Jonno said. "And so is the dog. Don't worry about them. For now."

Relief surged through Tara's body. But it was short-lived. Because she could sense a "but" coming.

Jonno walked over to her. He crouched right opposite her. Stroked her face. Stroked the tears from her cheek. Not softly, and lovelessly. And it made her cringe inside.

He looked right at her, his breath sour, and she wondered how she'd ever fallen for this man. For this monster.

He smiled at her. A little something between his two from teeth. "He's okay for now. If he stays well away. But something tells me he won't be able to resist following the little trail I laid for him. A trail that leads right here."

Tara's stomach turned.

Jonno's smile widened even more. "And when he gets here. When he comes to the rescue... when he proves how loyal he really is... I think it's about time we all had a civilised, grown-up conversation. Don't you?"

She saw the slightly off look he gave her.

The way his eyes shifted like there was nothing behind them.

Or rather, like there was something behind them, and what was behind them was absolutely terrifying.

But it was only when he stood up that her fear really intensified.

When the horror of what was happening finally started to settle in.

Because for the first time, Tara saw what Jonno was holding tight in his shaking hand.

A hammer.

A heavy, blunt hammer.
And a smile on his face.

CHAPTER FORTY-TWO

Sam walked back towards the city and quickly realized what a shitty idea this was.

It was morning. Far sunnier than yesterday. Seemed like the storm had just decided it couldn't be arsed any longer and passed over. The ground was still soaking and absolutely drenched. Water flowed down the long suburban road back towards the centre of town. Harvey didn't seem to mind it. He always liked water, so it was probably a novelty for him.

But Sam's feet were freezing cold. What he'd give for a hot bath right now.

He smirked at that. Shook his head.

He might as well get the idea of a nice hot bath out of his mind.

He wasn't going to be having one any time soon.

If ever again.

He looked at the stacks of cars beside him as he walked. Some of them still had people inside, sleeping in here. A family of four, with two kids in the back, absolutely zonked. A man at the steering wheel, staring wide-eyed outside.

But the bulk of the people had left their cars now. Many had spent the night here, it seemed. But most of them were walking now.

Walking back towards the city.

The desperate migration back to the city, back to their homes.

The desperate fights for the last of the supplies.

It was going to be ugly.

And it was going to be nasty.

Especially when what remained of the police and the military stepped in and tried to instil some kind of order.

It wasn't going to be pleasant.

And he wanted to be far away from here when all that shit went down.

But then he tightened his grip on Tara's broken bracelet, and he felt a knot in his chest.

He wasn't sure what it was about her that had drawn him to follow her. But there was something. And it was more than just a damned sense of duty or responsibility.

He knew it was dangerous, even entertaining the thoughts he was entertaining.

He still hadn't forgiven himself for the past.

And he still felt like he had some kind of loyalty to Rebecca, somehow...

But then he knew he was being ridiculous. Even entertaining what he was entertaining when things were so shitty and when this city was clearly collapsing around him was ridiculous.

He knew he needed to get home.

But he was worried about Tara. Especially with that nutjob fella of hers on the loose.

And the sooner he got to Tara and helped her, he could get back home, at the end of the day.

He splashed through the water. He wasn't sure why he thought Tara needed help or why she was in danger. It was just a feeling he had. A hunch he had, based on the way he'd found that broken bracelet.

And it could be useless. It could be pointless. It could be all in vain.

She might've gone another way.

She might not want him to find her after all.

There were so many possibilities. And that was forgetting that his chances of finding her were practically nil anyway.

Arnside, didn't she say? That's where her parents were?

Well, that was the opposite bloody direction to where he was heading anyway.

He shook his head. Kept on walking.

The less he thought about things, the better.

He walked further down the slope leading back towards the city. There weren't as many people around here or as many cars around here. He could see the high-rises in the city ahead. It looked normal. Just like it always looked from a distance. Relatively sleepy, as cities went.

But then he knew it wouldn't be sleepy within.

He knew the panic that would be starting to grow.

He knew the unrest that was on the cusp of breaking out.

In the distance, in neighbouring towns, he saw smoke rising, and he knew Preston wouldn't be far off following.

He took a deep breath and started to walk further down that slope, throwing caution to the goddamned wind, when he saw something over to his right.

It was something that caught his eye for reasons he couldn't explain.

And he wasn't even entirely sure how relevant it was.

But the more he looked at it... the more he wondered.

He headed through the water, over towards the thing that'd caught his eye.

And as much as he wondered, as much as he doubted it, as much as he questioned his judgement... he started to wonder if it might be something after all.

Something significant.

Something very significant.

He reached down.

Picked it up.

And he turned it around in his hands.

And the more he looked at it, the more convinced he grew.

It was a trainer.

A Nike trainer. White. But it looked a little torn around the side with wear and tear.

And there was something red on it.

He raised it to his nose, and he sniffed it.

Not blood.

Wine.

He lowered the trainer, and he looked at the woods at the side of the road.

Harvey let out a whine, wagging his tail nervously like he was uncertain.

"Come on," Sam said, squinting into the trees. "Let's... let's go take a look."

And then he stepped off the road and into the woods.

He didn't know what he was walking towards.

But he had a feeling he was getting close.

CHAPTER FORTY-THREE

Jonno watched Tara's little bitch of a boyfriend approach the cabin, and he smiled.
He tightened his fingers around the hammer.
Looked back at Tara.
Saw the horror in her widening eyes.
Saw her trying to wriggle free of her ties.
Saw that look on her face.
And his smile grew even wider.
The world had changed.
She'd broken the rules.
And she was going to pay for it.
They were all going to pay for it.
He looked back around at this "Sam" approaching, and he took a deep breath.
"Here we go," he said.

CHAPTER FORTY-FOUR

Sam saw the cabin in the distance, and he had a funny feeling this might be the place.

It was quiet in the woods. Deathly quiet. A little rain was falling again now. Clouds had filled the sky. There was a cool chill to the air. He could smell smoke in the distance somewhere. His stomach kept lurching for some kind of food, some substance, but he didn't think he'd be able to eat anything if he tried. He definitely didn't have an appetite right now.

Especially not with this cabin ahead of him.

It was a strange place. A rotted old cabin in the middle of the woods at the side of a country lane. He'd seen Tara's bracelet torn, and he'd headed back towards the city, as crazy as he knew that made him.

And then he'd seen her trainer, abandoned at the side of the road. Or *a* trainer, anyway. Because there was no proving it was hers. There was no knowing. Not for definite.

But that splash of red wine on top of it.

And now this cabin.

The footsteps leading towards it.

Something didn't feel right.

Something made Sam think this might just be the place.

Something made Sam worry about what he was going to find here.

Probably nothing at all.

He took a deep breath, his stomach turning with nerves.

He looked down at Harvey, whose ears pricked up. He seemed intrigued by his surroundings. Like something was catching his attention.

He looked back over his shoulder.

Back towards the road.

He saw the trees, thick, blocking his view of the road.

And around him, he saw nothing else but trees.

Nobody else.

He walked slowly towards the cabin. His footsteps crunched against the fallen tree branches, snapping them on contact. He kept on seeing movement in the corners of his eyes. But every time he looked, he'd just see a bird flying past. Or nothing at all.

His heart thumped. His nerves felt heightened. His entire sense of awareness felt heightened.

He had to get inside that cabin.

He had to search it.

For any more traces of Tara.

As long a shot as it was... it was the only choice he had right now.

He walked further towards the cabin when he saw something on the ground before him.

Something that made him freeze.

Footprints.

Footprints and a little mound of mud, upturned.

Sam was no expert.

But it looked like someone had been dragged along...

He remembered Iraq again.

Going inside that building.

Trying to get them out.

Dragging them through the sand...

He shook his head.

Took a sharp breath in.

Closed his eyes, just for a moment.

And then he let that breath go, and he turned back around to the cabin.

He didn't know what he was going to find.

And he couldn't be sure.

Not until he got in there and investigated for himself.

He walked further towards that cabin.

Further alongside those footprints.

The birdsong growing louder.

But the silence around that birdsong growing ever more... haunting.

He walked right up to the cabin door.

Stopped outside it.

It was a strange cabin. Dusty windows. Impossible to see inside. Mould growing all up the walls. Sam could smell the damp from here and the rotten wood.

He stood there, and he looked around again.

Looked all around.

Still nobody in sight.

He looked back at the cabin.

And then he climbed up the creaky steps.

The closer he got to the cabin door, the more he started to wonder if this was the right decision, and the more his instincts screamed at him to turn away. The more they shouted at him to go back. To leave here. Because this was stupid. This was insanity. He needed to get home. He needed to get home and start preparing for whatever the first week of the blackout held in store.

And then the first two weeks.

The first month.

The first year.

He had no idea how long this shit was going to last. But it was going to pay to be cautious, that was for sure.

He looked at that door, and he thought about Tara.

Thought about how she'd just disappeared after they'd... well, they'd shared a moment.

Disappeared into thin air.

Lost her bracelet.

Lost her trainer.

He had a bad feeling about her. A bad feeling that she hadn't just walked away after all. A bad feeling that something had happened to her.

And he wasn't going to just leave her behind.

He grabbed the rusty handle to the cabin door.

"Here goes nothing, Harv."

He lowered the handle, and he pushed open the cabin door.

It was dark and dusty in here. Damp, too. Really damp. He saw spiders scuttling around the second the light entered the cabin. Felt cobwebs against his face. Tasted the humidity in the air.

But all those slipped into the background.

All those slipped right into the background when he saw what was opposite.

When he saw *who* was opposite.

Across the cabin, tied up, gag around her mouth, he saw her.

"Tara," he said.

He rushed inside the cabin.

Saw her shaking her head. Looked like her eyes were streaming. Looked like she'd been crying.

"Holy hell," he muttered, trying to untie her wrists and going to pull the gag from her mouth. "It's alright. I'm—I'm here. Let's get you out of here. Let's—"

"Watch out!" she shouted. Right as he dragged the gag away from her mouth.

Sam frowned. "What..."

And then he heard it.

Footsteps.

Footsteps right behind him.

Creaking towards him.

Harvey barking.

He went to turn around.

But before he could, he felt it.

A heavy thump, right across his head.

Hard enough that it deafened him and made his ears ring.

He crumpled to the damp wooden floor.

Turned onto his back, his ears ringing, his head spinning.

And as Harvey barked away and stood his ground, Sam looked up and saw a man standing over him.

He was tall.

Well built.

He was holding a hammer.

And he had a smile on his face.

Jonno.

Tara's bastard ex.

It was him.

"Hello there," Jonno said. "How nice of you to join us."

Blood trickled from his hammer.

CHAPTER FORTY-FIVE

Sam felt the splitting pain burning through his skull, and he knew he was in deep, deep shit.

It was dark in this cabin, completely contrasting the brightness of outside. It was damp in here. He could smell it, thick in the air. In his mouth, he could taste the metallic tang of blood. His heart was racing. His body felt weak.

And his head ached and pulsated so, so bad.

That crack.

That hard crack over the head.

The hammer in Jonno's hand.

And Jonno standing there, staring down at him.

That smirk on his face.

That confident, arrogant smirk.

Harvey stood by Sam's side, kicking back, barking away. But Jonno didn't seem to notice him. He didn't seem to hear him at all.

All he noticed was Sam.

All he looked at with that anger in his bloodshot eyes was Sam.

"You really thought you could just wander away with my woman, and that'd be the end of it, did you?" Jonno asked.

Sam squinted around. His vision felt blurry.

He felt like he was on the brink of passing out at any given second.

But he couldn't pass out.

He couldn't *afford* to pass out.

He needed to stay conscious.

He needed to stay awake.

He was in danger.

Harvey was in danger.

And Tara was in danger.

He looked over at Tara, and his stomach sank. Tied there. Tears streaming down her face. Eyes wide and fearful. He was stupid for coming in here. Stupid for walking right into this trap.

"You should've stayed away," Jonno said. "Far, far away."

And then he walked right up to Sam and grabbed him by his hair.

"But I know how loyalty is," Jonno said. "And I know what it's like to think you're in love with someone. To want to protect them. I get it. Really, I do."

He squeezed his hands tight around Sam's head like a vice grip. And he smiled down at him. Looked right into his eyes and smiled.

"But you picked the wrong woman, matey," Jonno said. "And you picked the wrong man to fuck with."

And then he bashed Sam's head against the hard wooden floor.

"No!" Tara shouted.

Sam's head ached like mad. A splitting pain spread right through it. Another dizzy punch, making him want to pass out, making him want to drift away...

But he had to stay awake.

He had to keep on fighting.

Jonno looked around at Tara. He narrowed his eyes. Sam could see the disgust on his face. "You're begging for *him*? For this weak little piece of shit? Really?"

Tara shook her head. "Jonno, he's—he's not what you think he is. He hasn't done anything wrong—"

Another slam of his head, right against the wooden floor.

More barks from Harvey.

Those barks getting more aggressive now.

More protective.

Stay out of this, Harv.

Please, please stay out of this.

Don't antagonise this lunatic even more.

Jonno grabbed Sam's hair, then. He pulled him up, so he was looking right into his eyes. And Sam could see this man was too far gone. He could see the bloodshot little red worms on the whites of his eyes. He could see the froth at the corners of his mouth.

He could see the face of a man who felt like he had nothing left to lose.

A kid with a toy box and a whole world of ideas about what to do with it.

"You cross me, and you pay for it. That's something you're going to understand very soon."

And then he looked around at Tara.

"That's something you're *both* going to understand. Very soon."

A bolt of fear hit Sam square in the chest.

Because he knew what Jonno was implying.

He could see the lost look in this man's eyes, and he knew that he was implying something bad.

Really bad.

Violence.

He listened to Harvey barking away beside him as that crippling pain kept on bursting through his skull.

And he begged Harvey to stop.

He prayed he'd stop.

Because Jonno didn't look like a man who would stop for anybody.

He didn't look like a man who would suddenly realise the error of his ways and come back to the light side.

He stood there, shaking. His jaw kept on tightening and then loosening. Sweat trickled down his face. The vein in his temple was green, bulging, throbbing.

"You think you know her, don't you?" Jonno said.

"Jonno," Tara said. "Please—"

"You think you know her, but you don't. Not like I do. Oh, there's a lot about her past I'm sure she's keeping *well* hidden from you."

He looked up at her and smirked. Like his knowledge was a weapon, and he was on the verge of pulling the trigger.

And then he looked back at Sam. Shook his head. "Look at you. You were pathetic when I dragged you out of your car yesterday, and you're pathetic today. Only difference today is... there's no power. And there's no police out there to stop me. Will *someone* shut that *damned* dog up?"

He launched up then.

Stepped over towards Harvey.

Pulled back his hammer and held it over him while Harvey stood his ground and barked at him.

Saliva splashing from his jaws.

Bright, sharp white teeth on show.

Hairs on his back standing right on end.

But Jonno standing over him.

Hammer raised.

He looked at Sam.

Looked at him while he held that hammer over his dog's head.

And then he smirked.

Smirked, clearly at the power he had right now.

"Any last words for your mutt?" he asked.

Sam opened his mouth, but he couldn't say a word.

He felt weak.

Weak because of the agony in his head.

Weak because of the shaking of his body.

And weak because this man was threatening to take away his best friend.

His *only* friend.

And then Jonno just shook his head, and he smirked. "No? Never mind."

And then he took a deep breath and brought the hammer crashing right down towards Harvey's skull.

CHAPTER FORTY-SIX

Sam watched Jonno's hammer swing down towards Harvey's barking face, and his entire world stood still.

He lost all sense of time. All sense of space. All sense of *everything*.

And at that moment, all that mattered was Harvey.

All that mattered was his dog.

His loyal dog.

His best friend.

He watched the hammer move towards his skull in slow motion, and he wanted to get up.

He wanted to get to his feet, and he wanted to throw himself in front of it.

He wanted to *fight*.

And as he watched that hammer get closer and closer, time standing still, he didn't just see Harvey, but he saw the people in Iraq.

His comrades.

And those innocent families.

All trapped.

All crying out.

All begging for help.

Help us! Please help us! Please...

And then, out of nowhere, that hammer dropped to the floor.

It didn't slam against Harvey's head.

It didn't crack his skull.

It just fell from Jonno's fingers and hit the floor.

And Sam crouched there, and he felt relief. Total relief.

But also shock, too.

Shock because he wasn't expecting that to happen.

Shock because he thought Harvey was finished.

He thought Harvey was gone.

Shock because Jonno had dropped that hammer.

He'd dropped it, and Harvey was still barking.

He wasn't yelping as he'd pictured.

He was alive.

He was still alive.

Jonno looked down at Harvey and then back at Sam. He laughed a little. Shook his head. "You really think I'd hurt a dog?" He looked around at Tara then. "Really? Come on, Tara. Both of us know I'm not the violent one here."

Another wave of relief crashed into Sam. A wave of relief, but also pain. Because he was still shocked. He was still in disbelief.

This bastard was getting the better of him.

This bastard was *toying* with him.

And that wasn't right.

That wasn't right at all.

Jonno smiled and shook his head. And then he walked across the room, over to Tara.

The closer he got to Tara, the tenser Sam felt.

Because he felt this defensiveness.

He felt this sense of protectiveness.

He felt it, strong, and there was no way he was going to allow this creep to put his hands on her.

Not again.

"Look at you," Jonno said. "Sitting there like you're afraid. Sitting there like you don't know me. Sitting there with those crocodile tears. Sitting there like *you're* the victim. When we both know it's not you who's the victim. It never has been you who's the victim."

"Please," Tara said, shaking her head. "Don't."

"Don't what?" Jonno asked. "Tell him the truth? Why would that be? You worry he might see you differently if he knows? You worry he might judge you if he finds out what you are? What you're capable of?"

Tara glared over at Sam. And for the first time since he'd met her... she looked really vulnerable. Really uncomfortable.

And she looked afraid.

Very afraid.

"Isn't it about time we started being honest?" Jonno asked. "About everything? About why we're here? About the things we've done? And maybe then... maybe then we can *actually* make some progress. We can actually resolve some of our differences."

He looked at Sam, and he smiled.

And then he grabbed Tara by her hair.

Hard.

She let out a little wince as he pulled hard on her hair. Scrunched up her face. Looked like she was hurting. Looked like she was in pain.

He pulled her head up. And then he crouched right beside her. Kissed her on the cheek, something she clearly hated. And then he looked right back at Sam again. "Why don't you just be honest, hmm? Why don't you just tell him what you are? And what you've done?"

Sam could see the visible pain on Tara's face.

But it wasn't so much physical pain as it was emotional pain.

Pain over something she'd done.

Pain over something she was trying to hide.

Something she was trying to resist.

Something she was trying to suppress.

"Leave her the fuck alone," Sam said.

Jonno smirked as he gripped hold of Tara's mouth. Shook his head. "You don't get to make the orders here, fella."

Sam dragged himself to his feet. Stood up, a little shaky, a little wobbly, a little dizzy. And the pain in his head so intense, so strong. But standing. Standing.

For now.

He took a deep breath, and he looked right into Jonno's eyes. "I won't tell you again. Let her go."

"Or what? What're you gonna do, big man? Because if you come another step towards me, you're getting a hammer right in your skull. And this time... this time, I'll make sure you don't get up again."

Sam tensed his fists. Tried to stay steady on his feet.

He looked at Jonno, and he looked at Tara, and he listened to Harvey barking away, and he felt like he didn't have any option.

Like he didn't have a choice.

"Walk away. Right now. You walk away right now, and I might just go easy on you. Because this isn't any of your business, buddy. I have my issues with you. Oh boy, do I have my issues with you. But this... this isn't your fight. So I'll have more respect for you if you walk away."

Walk away.

Sam felt that urge.

He felt that instinctive urge to walk.

That instinctive urge to run.

Because Jonno was right.

This wasn't his battle.

This wasn't his fight.

But then... what was he supposed to do?

Just walk away?

Just leave this woman?

Leave Tara?

No. Like hell was he going to do that.

Jonno tightened his grip on Tara's hair.

And then he lifted his knife, and he pointed it right at Sam.

"You leave us to it, right now. You leave us to our shit. We're a couple, and we have things to talk about. Things to discuss. Things that don't concern you. So you walk away. You walk away right now. And take your yapping dog with you. And like I said. Maybe... maybe you and I can talk things out like grown-ups."

Sam opened his mouth to say something—something not nice—and then he remembered something.

In a bolt of a memory, he remembered something suddenly.

The rucksack.

The rucksack on the floor behind him.

What was in there.

The shotgun.

The shotgun he'd taken from Jeff.

He looked down at that rucksack by the door, and the hairs on his arms stood on end.

His heart started beating a little faster.

And then he looked back up at Jonno.

At Tara.

He looked at the pair of them, and as the adrenaline started to take hold... he realised he *did* have a choice after all.

He had a choice, and he knew what to do.

Exactly what to do.

He took another deep breath.

And then he nodded.

Half-smiled.

"Like you said," he said. "Family business."

He looked right into Tara's eyes when he said those words, and he saw the disappointment there.

He saw the look of betrayal on her face, and he felt so bad for her.

So bad about the horror she'd be feeling, just for a moment.

He looked at her a little longer, and he knew what he had to do.

You'll thank me for this in a moment. I promise you'll thank me for it.

He expected Jonno to smile. Expected him to nod and applaud or something dramatic like that.

But instead... instead, he narrowed his eyes.

He looked sceptical.

Unsure.

Like he didn't expect this.

And Sam knew he had to seize the moment.

He knew he had to get to that rucksack.

While he still had a chance.

He turned around and looked away from Tara, and he started walking towards the door.

And towards the rucksack.

He picked up his pace. Trying not to give himself away.

Trying not to give *anything* away.

He just had to get to that rucksack.

If he got to that rucksack, everything would be okay.

He walked towards it and went to crouch down and grab it.

"Leave the bag," Jonno said.

Sam stopped. His stomach sank. Shit. He was onto him.

But he couldn't let him stop him.

"I'm taking my supplies," Sam said.

He walked towards the rucksack again and reached down for it, so close to opening the zip.

"No," Jonno shouted.

And then he heard something that made his stomach turn cold.

Behind him, he heard Tara let out a cry.

He stopped.

Stopped, as much as he wanted to open that rucksack.

As much as he wanted to reach inside it.

As much as he wanted to grab that shotgun.

Because he couldn't risk anything happening to Tara.

He turned around slowly, and his stomach sank even further.

Jonno had the knife to Tara's throat.

It was pressed so hard against her neck that Sam could see blood trickling down it already and onto her white shirt.

Jonno's eyes were wide. More bloodshot than ever.

And the sweat was trickling off his face.

Blood oozing from the wound on his skull.

"You don't move another inch towards that rucksack," Jonno said. "Or she's dead. I promise you; she's dead. Understand?"

CHAPTER FORTY-SEVEN

Tara felt the blade pressing hard against her throat, and she was growing more and more certain that the end of her life was approaching—fast.

And she was beginning to wish she'd cracked Jonno over the head with that wine bottle a little harder.

Outside, it was light. A little rain was falling now, but nowhere near as much as yesterday. It looked like another storm was on the horizon. Like this was just a moment's brief respite from the new status quo, and everything was going to go to shit again very soon.

But Tara wasn't even sure she would be around to witness that new storm.

She felt the sharp blade pressing right against her throat. Her neck stung like he'd cut her already. His hand was shaking. But it was pressing against her hard. So hard that she was struggling to breathe properly.

And she could see from the look on Sam's face that this was serious. That he wasn't messing about.

She could see how he looked at her, wide-eyed like he was scared.

Like he was afraid.

"You don't move another muscle towards that rucksack," Jonno said. "Or I'll slit her throat. And don't think I won't."

He'd do that to her? Really? After all their years together and all those bold proclamations about how much he loved her, he'd just cut her throat right here—all because of a man wanting to be reunited with his rucksack?

That's all she meant to him?

But then, of course, that was the case. Of course, Jonno was the kind of psycho that would take a "she's mine or she's nobody's" attitude. She'd known he was that kind of creep for a long time now. She was his entire world—and not in a nice way. In a creepy way. In a controlling way.

But it was one thing to *know* it and another thing to *experience* the levels that went to first-hand.

And right now, she was fearing for her life.

Right now, she truly believed he was capable of killing her, right here.

Right now, she felt the end getting closer.

And there was nothing she could do about it.

"I just want to take my stuff," Sam said. Truth be told, Tara had been pretty mortified when Sam decided to just turn around and walk.

But now he was so adamantly trying to get to that rucksack… she could tell something else was going on here.

That he wasn't just walking away from her.

That he had a plan in mind.

He'd come all this way for her, after all.

He'd come all this way for her when Jonno had taken her away.

That had to count for something.

He wasn't just going to walk away from her again.

Jonno tightened that knife on her neck again. So hard now that it made her gag.

"I don't care what you want. In fact, you know what? You

should kick that rucksack over here right this second. Or she's finished. I promise you; she's finished."

Sam looked frozen. And it was abundantly clear there was something in that rucksack now. Blatantly obvious he had something in there that he knew might be able to help. She didn't know what, but clearly, he had something.

He looked down at the rucksack.

And then back up at Jonno.

Back at Tara.

Sadness in his eyes.

Jonno pushed the blade even further in.

So hard now that Tara could feel that wound on her neck opening up.

Stretching wider.

And yet, despite the pain, despite the fear for her own life, it was something else that she feared more than anything.

Her secret.

The secret Jonno kept threatening to unearth.

A secret he'd sworn to keep.

A secret she'd told him in the early days because she'd spent enough of her life burying her head in the sand and ignoring it.

But a secret that she felt comfortable enough opening up to Jonno about.

And a secret that he hadn't judged her for.

And that was part of why she loved him.

And now, here he was. The greatest betrayal. Threatening to use that secret against her, even though he swore he never would.

He was truly a monster.

And she regretted ever meeting him.

"Kick the rucksack over here," Jonno said. "Right now."

Sam was silent. "It's probably a bit heavy for that."

"Well, throw it here, then."

"Throw it? There's... there's a few fragile—"

"Fella, I don't care if your mum's finest fucking china is in there. Throw that rucksack over here, or she's done. I'm not playing around with this shit much longer."

And he wasn't playing.

He really wasn't playing.

And it made Tara feel so defenceless.

It made her feel so weak.

Because here she was. Relying on someone else to bail her out of a shitty situation.

A situation of her own making.

It was about time she stood up for herself.

It was about time she tried to fight for herself.

"Okay," Sam said, crouching down. "Okay…"

"But no funny business," Jonno barked. Adjusting the blade and cutting her neck a little higher up. "No funny business, or she's done. Do you really want that on your conscience?"

"Don't talk to me about conscience," Sam muttered.

"What was that?"

"Nothing," he said.

He crouched down, then. Grabbed the rucksack by its sides.

Tara's heart raced.

Jonno's hand shook as it pressed hard against her throat.

"Slowly," Jonno said. "Slowly. And then you throw it over here. Right now."

Sam looked Tara right in her eyes.

And then he muttered something.

He muttered something under his breath.

Something silent.

Something she didn't quite catch.

Not right away.

And then, as he looked deeply into her eyes, he was all she saw.

He was the only thing that existed, just for that sole moment.

"Be ready," he mouthed.

And then he stood up.

Pulled back the rucksack.

And he threw it towards Jonno.

Threw it as hard as he could.

The rucksack flew across the room.

Jonno pulled the knife away from her neck, instinctively, just for a split second, as the rucksack hurled through the air.

And Tara knew she had to try something.

She knew she couldn't just sit here.

She knew she couldn't just leave this all to Sam.

So she bit down on Jonno's hand.

Bit down.

Hard.

Jonno let out a cry.

A cry, as she sunk her teeth into the skin on his palms.

As she tore her teeth into his flesh.

As she tasted blood.

"Let go! Let go, you stupid bitch! Let go!"

He screamed out and punched at her head as she dug her teeth further into his skin.

As years' worth of anger spilled out.

As years' worth of rage poured out in that clenched jaw.

She watched Sam run across the room towards Jonno.

She watched Harvey race alongside him, barking.

She watched as she sunk her teeth further in, tasting warm blood all over her mouth, all over her lips.

And then she saw Sam grab Jonno and drag him to the floor.

Push him back, away from Tara.

Hard.

She felt the flesh tear from his palm.

And when he fell away, she tasted it in her mouth.

Jonno lay there on the floor, crying out.

Sam pinned him down, leg on his neck, as Harvey barked at him.

"Bitch!" Jonno shouted. "Murderous bitch!"

Murderous bitch...

She heard those words, and she remembered the water.

She remembered the glazed eyes.

She remembered the bubbles rising to the surface.

And the pain and the horror she'd felt.

All of it, rising to the surface of her mind...

Sam reached into the rucksack as Jonno bled out from his hand all over the floor. Harvey right beside him, barking at him, nipping his face.

And then Sam pulled out something from the rucksack that he must've been after all along.

A shotgun.

Some kind of shotgun.

He pointed it at Jonno's head with a possessed look in his eyes, and he pressed it down against his skull.

"Shut up," Sam shouted. "Right now. Or it'll be *you* who gets a bullet through your head."

CHAPTER FORTY-EIGHT

Sam held the gun to Jonno's head and had to use every inch of his self-control not to pull that fucking trigger.

Jonno crouched on the floor beneath him. He gripped onto his hand, which blood gushed out. Tara had bitten a chunk out of his hand. She'd really sunk her teeth into him. And sitting there, all pale-faced, blood trickling down her chin, she looked vampiric. She looked like a monster.

But he was so fucking glad she'd bitten that fucker.

He was so fucking glad.

Because Jonno deserved it.

All abusers deserved it.

Jonno clutched his hand. Blood spluttered out of his palm. He clenched his teeth together, wincing, gasping for breath. He looked in pain. Real pain. And Sam felt nothing about that. Not a flicker of sympathy.

The only thing he felt towards this man was anger.

Anger for how he'd dragged him out of his car yesterday like he was some kind of fucking big man.

Anger for how he'd threatened Tara.

Anger for chasing her down and kidnapping her.

And anger for threatening Harvey.

For using all of them like they were involved in some kind of fucked up game.

He looked down at Jonno, tickled his finger against the shotgun's trigger and wanted to pull it.

He wanted to fire.

He wanted to blow this fucker's brains all over this place.

And then he saw Jonno smirking up at him.

He was in pain. Clearly in pain.

But that look.

That smirk.

It was like he was getting some sort of kick from this.

Like he was enjoying it.

"Go on," Jonno said. "If you're so dead set on it, get it done. Pull that fucking trigger and get it done with."

Sam gritted his teeth. "Don't tempt me more than I already am."

Jonno laughed. And then he spat out a big blob of spit onto the floor between them both. "It'll make you two not so different. Ain't that right, Tara?"

Tara shook her head. She was still tied by her wrists. Blood trickling down her chin.

But she didn't look afraid anymore.

She didn't look defeated anymore.

She looked confident now.

Strong.

"Is this really what you want for me?" Jonno asked. "You want me to beg for my life right here? You want me dead, darling? Really? After everything we've been through? After everything we've done for you?"

Tara narrowed her eyes. Glanced at Sam. And for a moment, he worried. Worried this abusive fuck might worm his way into her head. Might convince her to try and talk him out of this.

And then he saw her inhale, right into her lungs. "The only

thing you've done for me is fuck up my life. I wish I'd never laid eyes on you, you abusive, manipulative, weak piece of shit. And I hope whatever happens here, you rot in hell."

Jonno stared up at her. His smirk slipped. Sam could see from how he looked at her that he wasn't expecting that. That he wasn't expecting her to speak so frankly. To say something so cutting.

But then he saw Jonno nod. Saw him look down at the floor as his hand bled out all over the place. "That's how it is. I see. After... after everything, that's how it is. That's how we've ended up—"

"Because of *you*," Tara said.

"Because of me?" Jonno said. Puffing his lips out in disbelief. "Really? I'm the only person in the world who stood by you. And I'm the only person in the world who *would* stand by you. Knowing what I know about you."

"And you used it against me," she said. "You used... you used what you knew to control me. And it embarrasses me. It fills me with shame. More than anything. Because... because I lost my strength. I lost all sense of who I was. I became exactly what I'd spent my life trying not to be. Reliant. Reliant on somebody else. And I... I can see where I've gone wrong there now. I can see where I've doubted myself and where it's held me back. But—but it ends. It ends right now. And whatever happens here... whatever you have to say... it's on you."

Jonno looked over at her. Looked at her looking so defiant. So confident. So self-assured.

And then he looked around at Sam.

Looked right into his eyes.

And it was only then that Sam saw he was crying.

"You really want to know what she is?" Jonno said. "Exactly what she is? And exactly why I'm the only one who'd stand by her? You really want that, buddy?"

Sam looked down at Jonno, and he narrowed his eyes.

And then he looked at Tara.

Saw her, tearful.

But confident.

Standing her ground.

Jonno's blood drying on her chin.

"You want to know what she's capable of?" Jonno said. "You want to know what a monster she is? Okay. How about I tell you everything. Right from the start."

Sam looked up at Tara.

He looked right into her eyes, and she looked back at him.

And he saw that vulnerability.

He saw that openness.

He saw that trepidation and that tension, and he saw the look of a woman who was about to be set free.

Terrified, but about to be set free.

And then he looked back at Jonno as he held onto that shotgun, and he shook his head.

"I really couldn't give a shit about her past," he said.

Jonno's eyes narrowed. "What—"

And then Sam pulled back the shotgun and cracked him across the head.

Hard.

Hard enough to send him falling to the floor.

Hard enough to leave him lying there, twitching, frothing at the mouth.

Saliva dribbled down Jonno's chin. His eyes rolled back into his skull. His body shook and convulsed.

And Sam didn't feel anything.

He didn't feel ashamed of what he'd done.

He didn't feel any pity for this man.

He just felt like he'd done the right thing.

The only thing.

He walked over to Tara, his head still splitting with pain.

He reached into his rucksack, and he pulled out some scissors. Cut her free.

Then he reached further into the rucksack and pulled out some dental floss.

"Told you this would come in handy," he said.

Tara smiled. Crying but smiling.

And then he cut the ties around her ankles.

Cut the ties around her wrists.

And when she was free, she fell into his arms.

She hugged him. Close.

And he stood there awkwardly. The warmth of her body pressing against his. And it felt nice. He couldn't remember the last time someone had hugged him. The last time someone held him like this.

He rested his arms on her back for a second, letting himself sink into that warmth.

He looked down at Jonno lying there, unconscious on the floor. Bleeding from his hand and his head.

He took a deep breath, and he swallowed a lump in his throat.

"Come on," he said. "Let's get out of here. Let's... let's go home."

CHAPTER FORTY-NINE

Sam couldn't describe the relief he felt when he saw his home looming in the distance.

He was at the top of his road. There wasn't much traffic on the road he lived on. Never was. Pretty quiet road that ran right through a bunch of fields and farmland. So it was ideal, really. A perfect respite from the chaos surrounding. From the cars stacked up behind one another. From the urban areas full of people wondering what the hell was going on and what would happen next.

And it scared him. Knowing the state the city was going to be in today. Knowing the panic people were going to be going through and experiencing. People displaced far from home. People realising they had no water. People realising they had no food.

And people realising they had nobody to tell them what to do next.

And that was perhaps the scariest thing of all.

Those people who were woefully underprepared for all this.

Which accounted for most of the population.

They were in for a shock.

The biggest shock of all.

And it was important Sam just took things one step at a time.

He didn't know how long all this was going to last. He didn't know what happened next.

Just that this wasn't going to be an easy journey ahead.

Even if the power did come back on soon... the country had changed.

The world had changed.

And *his* world had changed.

He looked to his right and saw Tara walking alongside him and Harvey. He felt a little nervous about seeing her there. A little uncomfortable. It still wasn't natural for him to be walking so close to someone else.

She wasn't talking. Wasn't saying much. She just kept up glancing up at him. And then occasionally back over her shoulder. A look of guilt in her eyes.

"Don't worry," Sam said. "He's not coming after you. Not this time."

Tara turned back to him and raised an eyebrow. "You said that last time. And he found us. Who's to say he won't find us again?"

Sam thought back to how they'd left Jonno. Tied up in that chair, back in that cabin in the middle of the woods. Gagged. It was brutal. Savage. But he had no regrets about leaving him there like that.

He'd terrorised Tara. He'd threatened him and Harvey.

He deserved no better than that.

"Something just tells me he won't be bothering us again," Sam said.

Tara nodded. But she seemed distant. And as much as Sam didn't want to pry... he sensed something had unsettled her. And he had a funny feeling it wasn't the fact they'd just left her ex-boyfriend for dead.

It was something he'd said.

Something about her past.

He looked at her as she looked back at him, and he wanted her to open up.

He looked into those blue eyes—the window to her soul—and he wanted to know about her.

Everything about her.

"I was in Iraq five years ago," Sam said. "Army. I... was on a scouting mission in a small town. We were told there were insurgents everywhere. The group I were with... they weren't a good bunch. Not at all. They used to boast about how many people they'd killed. Chat about how they'd murder innocent families and then leave spare rifles with them, all to make it look like they were just defending themselves.

"And I... I didn't want to get involved. I didn't want to think about it. I wanted to just bury my head in the sand and get on with the job. Until one day I found myself in... I found myself in a situation with four of them."

Sam swallowed a lump in his throat.

His heart racing faster.

Speak.

Let it out.

Let the truth out.

It's time.

He closed his eyes, and he braced himself for the moment his whole life had been building up towards.

"You don't have to," Tara said.

But Sam didn't listen. "They... they found this family. Man. Woman. Kids. Two of them. Two little boys. And an old woman, too. And I'd heard the rumours about them. Yannis, the main guy was called. I'd heard the rumours about how brutal he was. How savage he was. But still, you never expect to actually witness something like that until... well. Until you actually witness it, right?"

Tara nodded. Listening. Not judging. Just listening.

"I... I saw Yannis lift the rifle and point it at the old woman.

Put a bullet through her head. I saw... I saw this family screaming. Begging. And I saw the group I was with and I... I just couldn't let it happen. And I knew... I knew there'd be a better way. And I knew there had to be a better solution. But I..."

Please. Please help us. Please!

He closed his eyes, and he was there again.

The smell of sweat and delicious spices in this living room.

The heat in this thick military outfit.

The sound of dogs barking and chickens clucking outside.

And the sight of this family, all on their knees.

Yannis standing in front of them.

Two of his arse-lickers either side of him.

"Shoot one of 'em, Sam," Yannis said. "Go on. Don't be a pussy. They're all terrorist sympathisers anyway. Just shoot one of 'em."

And he'd stood there with the rifle in his hand, heart racing.

He'd looked down into the father's eyes. Into his broken glasses. At the tears rolling down his face.

"Please," he said. "Don't do this. Don't let us die. Please help us. Please."

Sam looked down at that man, and he wished he could do something to help him.

He wished he could do *anything* just to end this situation—this mess.

But he knew what the consequences were if he didn't shoot.

He'd probably wind up shot himself.

Because he was in on the secret now.

"Go on, Sam," Yannis barked. "What the hell's holdin' you back?"

And Sam didn't want to do it.

He didn't want to pull that trigger.

He stood there and his heart raced and the heat grew more intense and the screaming and the begging grew even louder and—

"Do it!" Yannis barked.

So Sam lifted the rifle.

He pointed it at Yannis.

And he pulled the trigger.

"I'll never forget the look on Yannis's face when that bullet split his skull," Sam said. "The way he looked at me. It was like... like he was staring right into my soul. Like he was promising to haunt me. Pledging to curse me for the rest of my life."

Tara stared back at Sam. Her eyes were tearing up. "What happened next?"

Sam sighed. "I... I put down the gun. Two of Yannis's lackeys took me back to camp and grassed on me. I was discharged and immediately kicked out. I was put on trial, and I was found not guilty on grounds of insufficient evidence. I have no idea what happened to that family. But I... I don't know. Some sentimental part of me likes to think they were looking out for me when that verdict came through."

Tara shook her head. "It wasn't... it wasn't your fault. That monster. He would've killed them."

"My life didn't stop turning to shit then, though. My wife. Rebecca. Love of my life. I couldn't open up to her. I couldn't tell her how I was feeling. I... I couldn't even tell her the truth. About what happened. She kept telling me I needed... I needed therapy. But opening up... the thought of it made it feel like it would break me into pieces. I couldn't do it. I tried to keep it together. I tried to hold on to my sanity. I lost my mind. Got angry. Shouted. Said things I shouldn't have said, all because of these memories I had. All because of this guilt I had. *Have*. And in the end, everything around me fell away."

Tara just stared at Sam. Wide-eyed. Shaking her head.

"You're the first person I've ever told this to," Sam said. "You're the first person I've ever felt the courage and the comfort to open up to. I... It's not been easy. But it's not been as difficult as I thought it would. So thank you."

Tara just looked at him. And Sam worried she might judge him. She might have a different opinion of him. She might turn her back on him, and she might walk away.

But instead, she reached over to him.

She took his hand.

Squeezed it. Just a little.

Smiled.

"It's okay," she said. "I'm here. I'm... I'm here."

Sam looked into her eyes, and he felt a weight lifting from his shoulders. He smiled at her. "Thank you. And I'm... I'm here too."

Tara looked away. Opened her mouth. And he sensed she might be on the verge of opening up about something, too. Something just as heavy. Something just as deep.

And then she closed her mouth. Looked back at him. Right in his eyes.

"There's things... things from my past I'm not comfortable with either. Things I'm... still coming to terms with. And I will talk about them. One day, I will talk about them. But for now... can we just... can we just go back for one of those nice portable stove meals you told me about or something? Before I... before I hit the road again?"

Before I hit the road again...

He didn't know whether she was just saying that to test the waters.

He didn't know whether she was wanting him to say no, you're not hitting the road again—you're coming home.

Coming home with me.

But in the end, he just looked at her, right at her, and he smiled and nodded.

"That can be arranged," he said.

She smiled back at him. And he wondered what secrets she was hiding. What past she was keeping hidden.

One day, maybe, he'd find out.

Maybe.

But not today.

He turned around.

Looked down the road towards the little terraced cottage he called home.

"Come on then," he said. "Let's... let's get back."

Tara squeezed his hand once more.

And then she let go, and they walked down the road towards Sam's house.

He didn't know how things were going to go.

He knew the city had changed dramatically in this last day.

And he knew things were going to get worse before they got better.

But as he walked down the road towards his house, Harvey and Tara by his side, he found himself smiling.

He found himself hopeful.

Because he wasn't alone.

For now, for as long as it lasted, he wasn't alone.

CHAPTER FIFTY

Jonno sat in that chair with tears rolling down his cheeks, and he felt anger.

Pure anger, seething, burning through his body.

How had he been so stupid?

So fucking stupid as to let them get away.

So fucking stupid as to let that bitch and her fuck thing escape him.

So fucking stupid to end up tied up in this chair himself.

He tried to scream at the top of his lungs, but the gag they'd wrapped around his mouth stopped him from making a sound. He rocked on his chair, backwards and forwards, but it was really no use.

He was stuck here.

He was trapped here.

And he wasn't getting out of here.

He tried to yank the cuffs around his wrists apart but with no success. He knew how strong those cable ties were. He'd made sure they were tight around Tara's wrists not long ago at all.

Tara.

Bitch.

Absolute spawn of the fucking Devil.

Ungrateful cunt.

He should've made her pay.

He shouldn't have even given her a chance to speak out.

He should've bludgeoned that evil cunt's skull while he had the chance.

He sat there as tears ran down his face, and he thought of the better times they had together. The day they'd first met in that park. The day he'd seen her and thought she was the most beautiful woman he'd ever met.

The holidays they had.

Crispy pizza in Rome.

Too much wine and going back to their apartment and laughing together because he couldn't get an erection—and neither of them caring.

Both of them just so happy in each other's company.

Both of them just so comfortable.

So content.

He thought about those moments, and he wondered how they'd got so far from that, so suddenly.

Or rather... how things deteriorated as rapidly as they had.

What had they done to each other?

But no. It wasn't on him.

He was just trying to look out for her.

He knew what was best for her.

He knew what made her click, and he knew what was good for her.

He knew a lot more about Tara than anyone else.

And if he knew Tara like he thought he knew her... she wasn't going to be able to hide from him forever.

He sat there in that chair as the rain started hammering down again outside, and as much as he felt trapped here, as much as he felt stuck, he also felt a confidence.

A confidence that he was going to get out of here.

And a confidence that he was going to finish what he started.

Because a predator didn't just give up just because their prey had fled.

He was going to keep on going.

He was going to keep on hunting.

No matter what it took.

He closed his burning eyes, and instead of seeing Tara's face in his mind and feeling butterflies, he saw her dismembered head, and he felt happiness.

A smile crept across his face.

A smile at the thought of her lying in a pool of her own blood.

Of that cunt Sam beside her, and his dog hanging from a fucking leash.

His smile widened.

He could sit here all day.

He could wait all day.

Because eventually, someone was going to come in here.

Eventually, someone was going to find him.

And eventually—

"Holy hell."

Jonno opened his eyes.

Standing opposite him, he saw a man and a woman. They looked about in their forties. And they had a kid beside them. A young boy, by the looks of things.

"What the hell? Safia, take Eustice outside. He—he shouldn't see this."

The woman nodded, clearly shocked, and took the boy outside.

The man walked over to him. He searched the cabin, clearly nervous. "I—I'll get you out of there, sir. Don't you worry. Just... just bear with me a moment."

And as he searched the room for something he could use, Jonno felt his smile widening.

He felt his happiness growing.

He felt like all his prayers were being answered at once.

The man came over. Pair of hedge cutters in hand. "You hold still, okay? I don't—I don't want to end up catching you."

Jonno nodded. Trying to look rattled. Trying to look shaken up. Trying to look like the victim...

No. Wait. He didn't need to *look* like the victim.

He *was* the victim.

Right?

The man snapped the ties free from his wrists and ankles. And when he'd done that, he pulled the gag away from Jonno's mouth. "There you go. That... that should be better."

Jonno leaned forward and heaved all over the floor of the cabin.

Mostly for dramatic effect.

Mostly.

The man patted his back. Gently. "What... what on earth happened to you? Here. Let's—let's get you some water. You look like you could use some."

The man handed him some water, which Jonno sipped. The tastiest damned water he'd ever tasted.

And when he'd finished, he handed it back to the man. Nodded. "Thank you. I... You've no idea how much I appreciate that."

The man smiled at him. "Quite alright. Are—are you okay?"

Jonno looked into this man's kind eyes.

He looked out of the door towards the little boy, peeking around the corner.

And then he looked out at the rain.

Out at the trees.

Out into the distance, in the direction he'd watched Tara and Sam leave this place.

A smile stretched across his face.

"I am now," he said.

He was going to find them.

And he was going to make them rue the day they'd ever crossed him.

He was going to ring that bitch's fucking neck.

He was going to gut her.

He was going to end her fucking life.

No more fucking around.

It was time to make her suffer for what she'd done.

And then it was time to end her ungrateful life.

Slowly.

Painfully.

Delightfully.

END OF BOOK 1

Dawn of Darkness, the second book in the World Without Power series, is now available.

If you want to be notified when Ryan Casey's next novel is released—and receive an exclusive post apocalyptic novel totally free—sign up for the author newsletter: ryancaseybooks.com/fanclub

Printed in Great Britain
by Amazon